For anyone who ever inspired me to write.

Contents

ONE

Arson & Murder?

The first bottle smashed against the far wall and lit up the room with sheets of flame, the vodka inside igniting everywhere.

The fumes fuelled it and soon the whole place was burning. As the flames took hold, I lit the rag round the top of the second, grabbing it, hurling it towards the other wall and running back towards that door.

Distribution was dealt with. Now for Production.

I slammed the door behind me, hearing things start to blow up.

Bottle number three smashed in the corner and flames went up to the roof, covering the stills in thick black smoke.

I only had seconds to get out of there.

Yeah, I knew that, but I couldn't move.

I couldn't take my eyes off it all.

Couldn't believe what I was seeing, what was happening.

It was only when that smoke reached me, my eyes began stinging and I struggled to get my breath that my brain started working.

Out through that door, shutting it behind me and walking over to where we'd struggled a few minutes ago, shining my torch down on the body.

The *body*.

No longer a person, no.

Now he was a corpse, a dead man, a murder victim.

His dead eyes still gazed up at me, like they were accusing me of it.

But I hadn't killed him.

Had I?

I couldn't have, not me.

No way, I wasn't a murderer.

Reaching into my bag, I got the last bottle out, wrapped the last rag round it and knelt to set it on fire.

I turned the torch off and picked up my balaclava from the floor.

"Sorry mate," I murmured, as something exploded next door and the whole building shook. "It weren't me, honestly. It were him."

Grabbing the bottle with the flaming top, I ran to the door leading to the stairs and turned to look at this room one last time. This room with my dead mate lying on his back in the centre.

Fuck it, I thought, hurling the bottle as hard as I could onto the stone floor. It wasn't me, I wasn't a murderer.

Not yet anyway.

Two

The Man From *Motown Cop*

"Are you joking? Seriously Melanie, are you bloody joking? Who does it bleeding well sound like?"

"Now there's no need for that, sir…"

"It's *Luke*. Jesus, Mel, you…"

"Oh Luke," she said, sounding relieved. "I can't hear you with that music on."

"Hang on."

He put his hand over the mouthpiece and leant round the door, nodding to the barman. "Oi mate, turn it down a bit. I can hardly hear myself speak."

"Not your pub is it, chief?"

He sighed. "Alright. Please could you turn the radio down slightly? I am paying for this call, y'know? Two minutes, yeah? Then you can whack it up as high as you like and we'll all have a dance."

Bloody Sparks being that loud at eleven in the morning.

Jesus, he hadn't missed this place one bit.

The barman turned the knob and the two coalmen at the bar glared at Heslin, trying to look tough with their sooty faces.

"Mel, you there?"

"Still here. Look, where are you?"

"Never mind. Listen, I need to speak to him. Is he there? Please tell me he's there."

"He's out to lunch."

"Bullshit, Mel, he's told you to tell me that. It's only just gone eleven. No-one goes to lunch at that time. Now get him on the telephone."

"Luke, honestly…"

"Is he avoiding me?"

"Luke…"

"For God's sake, just tell me, right? We're mates, yeah? So just tell me right out: how much trouble am I in? Can he smooth it over? I can't afford to lose all this, yeah? I can't. I've worked hard and I'll do whatever Sid wants, just don't let…"

"I'll do what I can," she said. "I'll speak to Dean when I see him and try to find out what's gonna happen."

"Mel…?"

"But I wouldn't hold your breath. There's been talk of a slander charge. You could wind up in court. Fined."

"Shit."

"There isn't much I can do, is there?"

"That bloody journo stitched me up, Mel. Tell Dean that. Get him to tell Sid today. *Today*. Look, *is* Dean there?"

He had a sweat on now. Slander, court. Christ, it got worse. As if Thursday morning hadn't been bad enough.

"He's out to lunch. Call me later."

And she hung up on him.

Heslin poked his head round the door, rummaging for change, and caught the eye of the shorter coalman. "Come here," he said. "I need your help."

Those two looked at each other and the other went to say something smart when Heslin told his mate there was money in it for him.

"I need you to ring this number," he said, handing the paper over with some coins. "Ask for Dean Beckett. Tell whoever answers it's Mickey Fleming. That's you, yeah?"

The coalman didn't say anything. He just took the coins and dialled.

Heslin heard Melanie answer.

"Hi, yeah, it's er..."

He looked at Heslin, forgetting the name. Heslin mouthed it, muttering 'prick' at the end.

"Mickey Fleming. Dean Beckett around?"

"He is, Mickey, yes. Hang on," she was saying. "Dean?"

Heslin took the receiver and put it back. "Ignoring me," he muttered. "Thanks."

"Don't call me a prick again, alright?"

"Yeah, sorry."

Heslin followed him into the pub and asked for a pint of Outlaw. The radio – a bit of "Rebel Rebel" – went up loud before the barman poured the ale.

"Is out the back open?"

"Aye. There's benches there now."

Heslin almost smiled. Benches outside the Collier's Arms. As he walked to the door, one of the coalmen made a comment about his floral shirt and all three laughed.

God, he hadn't missed this place at all.

The pint made him feel a bit better but wasn't that always the case? It also made him drowsy and hungry so he let

5

himself out the back gate and went down Wroughton Street to see if that chippie was still there, relieved to see it was. It had a new front now. Well, a different front from the brown one he'd spent his teenage years standing outside. New staff too. The bird who always sounded stoned must be long gone.

Heslin took his food and sat on the church wall further down the street, watching the shop fronts, seeing a couple of Littlewoods birds showing leg in the August sunshine.

He was finished.

It was a bastard of an industry and there were rules to follow closely if you were to survive it. Yet the signs of him screwing up were all there too and God, that pissed him off. His drinking at Beckett's Christmas party had landed him in the shit – he'd had that prick from the West End telling him he needed to shut up and listen more. Jesus, even shy little Melanie had asked why he felt the need to shoot his mouth off whenever he wasn't the centre of attention. Piss off, Mel, he'd thought back then, if I wanna make myself known then that's what I'm gonna do.

Now he'd made himself known alright.

Lucas Heslin: soon to be famous for all the wrong reasons. He daren't even think about the calibre of those he'd pissed off. Or what they were capable of.

He'd worked his arse off to get where he'd got to and had no-one else to thank for whatever had come his way. Trouble was, he had no-one else to blame either when it all went wrong. As it was doing now – spectacularly.

Christ, he was ready to take up smoking again.

Heslin tipped the remaining chips on the floor and flicked through the greasy newspaper – Friday's *Daily Telegraph* – hoping to God he wasn't in it anywhere.

Nixon telling America 'I Resign', gift tax soon to be levied, a man from the BBC blown up in Cyprus and some Hitler Youth leader dying. They all featured but there was nothing about him and nothing about Sid. Yet.

He screwed up and dropped the paper and crossed to the telephone box, getting a glance from one of those tasty student birds as he passed. He thought, you'd better savour that, Lucas. The way your career's going there won't be many people recognising you from here on in.

Surprise surprise, Dean still wasn't taking his calls.

Mel told him to lie low, told him Dean was doing his best to square things with Sid, told him Dean was ringing his journo contacts to get them to kill the story – Dean telling them there *was* no story.

Heslin softly banged his head on the door a couple of times. He left Mel the number of his boarding house and hung up.

When he came out, he was dripping with sweat. Feeling in his pocket, he pulled out green aviators – a gift from Sid at the wrap party – stuck them on his nose and sauntered back up the road in a daze.

Mrs. Swallow's boarding house was only two streets away from where he'd grown up, his old man telling him as a kid it had a reputation that place. A place where bad men go when their wives kick them out. A place for exiles then, yeah? Perfect for him.

The old cow was polishing that same cabinet when he came through the door. She looked up, didn't acknowledge him.

He went up to his attic room, taking the second *Motown Cop* script from his suitcase and flicking through it for the hundredth time.

A few minutes later, he washed and lay down, telling himself he was finally finished as he closed his eyes.

Around four he got up, dressed in the same clothes and went out, asking the old cow if anyone had phoned.

It took five minutes to get to the Collier's Arms and another two to get noticed – the barman preferring conversation with his regulars to serving a paying customer.

"Outlaw. Two pints."

"Both for you?"

"I earn it."

"No problem, chief, I weren't saying owt."

"I thought I'd spend a couple of hours sitting on one of your glorious benches in the sun," he said drily.

"Aye, they get quite popular this time of year. Gives the old place an air of the continent, I say."

Heslin dropped coins on the bar and went out, thinking, as if you've ever been to the continent on your wage.

There were people out here now.

He went to the corner by the white brick wall and sat, putting his feet on the chair opposite and observing through his shades.

Three men – postmen? – in their navy blue sat playing dominoes and drinking halves.

A floppy-haired student was trying to make a bird with a pageboy laugh, not seeing that she really wasn't interested. The old Luke would have said something to him on his way out – 'Leave it out mate, she's not your type' – or something to humiliate him and make her smile.

But this Luke was learning. He wasn't gonna shoot his mouth off about any*thing* or any*one* anymore. He was gonna pinch himself every time he felt a smart remark coming.

The first pint went down beautifully, made him wanna telephone Mel and say sorry for swearing earlier.

An old couple in matching tweed came out and sat at a table, him opening *The Daily Mail* and her taking some knitting from her bag.

A coloured in dreads was by the gate.

Two hard men were talking in hushed tones and, like many pubs, a middle-aged woman, dressed up to the nines, drinking spirits and looking like she might start crying any minute, sat alone at a table.

This was how bad his situation was.

He'd had to come *home* to escape it.

Heslin had seen them all, or so he thought, as he raised his pint – all the characters drinking at half four on a Monday round the back of the Collier's Arms.

All except her.

How the Hell he'd missed her with his sweep of the plot, he didn't know.

How he'd not felt her gaze on him.

Sitting beneath a green umbrella at a table in the far corner, twenty feet away, there she was.

A proper lady, not a bird, not a scrubber, but an actual *lady* like you saw in London. The kind who'd make you have a bath before the *intercourse* started. Too classy for this dump.

She was wiping her huge shades and staring right at him, not blinking when he returned the gaze and not intimidated by him checking her out.

Heslin slowly removed his shades to get a better look.

She was in a brown jersey floral dress that came to her ankles, a wide orange belt at her midriff, flat sandals on her feet, legs crossed, bloody awesome breasts. Bare arms too and he had a thing for arms. On one wrist was what looked like a leather bracelet – the kind kids try to sell you abroad – and she wore a heavy silver chain around her neck.

Before she put her shades back on, still focussed on him – Luke Heslin drinking alone to get pissed – he got a good look at her eyes.

Very dark and narrow, made-up perfectly with tonnes of blue eyeshadow. She had straight brown hair falling to her shoulders, held back by an Alice band. Cute nose too.

He'd got used to noticing everything about people these last few years. An old luvvie had said it was the best training an actor could have. Screw acting, it made picking up birds much easier.

And she was *still* staring.

He watched her rummaging in her bag and then taking a long sip of her – what looked like – gin.

Heslin smiled and mouthed 'Hi', raising his hand in a pathetic wave.

This lady smiled back.

Yeah, she recognised him. One of the eleven million who'd caught it last month.

"Are you going to come over and chat me up?" she said. "Or are you going to sit and stare?"

He grabbed his pint, wished he'd changed his clothes, and passed the other drinkers who hadn't noticed he'd *just this second* pulled without effort.

"Sorry miss," he said, sitting opposite. "I'm used to women coming over to me to chat *me* up. It's a perk of the job."

He gave her a sheepish smile.

She took her shades off and laid them on the table. "I thought it was you. Lucas?"

He nodded.

"You went to my college."

"I did?"

"Chestnut Grove."

"Yeah, I went there. But I don't…"

"I'm a little older than you," she said softly.

"And you are? Your name, I mean. Not your age."

"Rebecca. Rebecca Rollins."

"Rebecca Rollins," he said, trying to remember. "I'm Luke, by the way. Not Lucas, not really. Can I get you a drink?"

"Not right now."

"That's strange, you knowing me from back then. For the last nine days, most people know me from…"

"*Motown Cop*," Rebecca said. "I thought they might. It was very good. Will there be more?"

He took a big drink while he thought how to answer that. Have a bit of faith, Lucas, he told himself silently.

"We've written the scripts. It starts shooting in a few months."

"I thought the coloured American was charming."

"Estes?"

"Is that his name?"

"Yeah, he's alright. Up his own arse really. Flash for a coloured…"

He stopped himself. What was wrong with him? Two and a half pints, one he'd slept off, and he was mouthing off again.

Rebecca smiled. "Well, he was a star on-screen anyway. She was very pretty too."

Heslin nodded, wondering whether to tell her or not, but deciding women didn't tend to be impressed by which other women men had slept with.

"Fay, yeah? Lovely girl. What did you think to the ending?"

"Loved it. So understated."

"We were shooting that when they let the bomb off on Westminster Bridge. I've never seen chaos like it."

"I can imagine," she said. "I saw it on the news."

There was a pause as they both took a drink.

"No offence," Heslin then said, "but I don't remember you from college. What year were you in?"

"All of them."

"No, I meant…"

"I left when I was eighteen. In sixty-two."

"You're thirty now?"

"And you're a brilliant mathematician, Luke. How old are you now?"

"Twenty-eight."

"Twenty-eight. A real-life movie star home for the weekend and I knew him when he was a boy."

"Not quite a movie star."

"But you've been in movies?"

He shrugged. "I tested for Bond in sixty-eight. They said I was too young and too blond so they went with Lazenby."

"Impressive. Have you met the others? Sean? Roger?"

"I was in *The Persuaders*. Roger's funny."

"Sean?"

"Nope."

"What else have you done?"

"Cyberman in *Doctor Who* and an embezzler in *Crown Court* last year. That's it for speaking parts. The Bond geezers liked my test and flew me out to Switzerland for *On Her Majesty's Secret Service*. I spent a fortnight freezing my arse off on a mountain with a Sten gun. Why are you smiling?"

"Is that why you wear shirts like that? To get noticed in crowd scenes?"

She was sharper than any others of late. Much tastier too and he couldn't wait to bury his head in those breasts. Get her nailed, get his career back on track – August seventy-four, one for his *Who's Who* entry.

"I like it…"

"It's nice, I'm joking," she said, putting her hand on his. She rested her chin in her other hand and looked him in the eyes.

"Finished with this, chief?" the barman called from behind Heslin.

He turned to see the barman holding his empty pint pot. "It looks like it, doesn't it?" Heslin said and turned back to see her smiling. "Why's he open at this time?"

"I heard he obtained an afternoon licence from the authority."

"How *continental*."

"Bless him. He's the only man in the whole town who's pro-Common Market," Rebecca said, taking a sip of her drink. They sat in silence until she said, "So what does bring you home?"

He took a deep breath and sighed. He might as well be honest. Honesty was hardly shooting his mouth off.

"I'm avoiding people. A lot of people."

She took it well, held his gaze, didn't seem surprised. "Why?"

"I did something stupid. Something so bloody stupid I'd kick myself in the balls for it if I could."

"Really?"

"Really. *Motown Cop*? The Wednesday after it went out – *last* Wednesday – I had a few drinks and ended up chatting to this journalist. The bastard stitched me up with loaded questions."

"You said something you shouldn't have?"

"You might say."

"Shall we continue this at my place? I have some Blue Nun."

Christ, she only wanted the gossip, that was all. But if he could get her pissed, he could nail her anyway. It wouldn't do any harm. Then she could tell all her friends when he'd fled that she'd spent the night with that geezer who was almost on the telly.

"Your place it is."

"But...," she began. "No."

"What?"

"I was going to say, don't leave me in suspense. What did you say? It can't have been that bad, surely?"

"Sidney King, he's our producer. Very powerful man. Have you heard of him?"

"I don't think so."

"Well, everyone in the trade has and they all know not to cross him. How can I put this? Erm... he's got a massive secret. There's rumours and all but they get quashed and the very few people who spread them end up doing a Pete Duel. That's the way I'm headed."

Rebecca stood up and looked down at him, a smile on her lips. She put her shades back on and folded her arms. "Rumours?"

"A journo had to get a lot of drink down my neck to find them out. Why would I tell you now?"

She shrugged. "I just think you will. You like to speak, don't you?"

"He's connected," Heslin said. "Do you know what that means?"

"Organised crime?"

"Yeah. Very organised and very criminal. One of the biggest firms in London."

"And you told a journalist that? Tut tut," she said, shaking her head.

"It was meant in confidence but bloody Hell, the way the telephone kept ringing on Wednesday, it obviously wasn't taken that way." He downed his pint. "I woke up on Thursday morning with two geezers stood over me. One smashed my two hundred-year-old mirror with a cricket bat. The other carved up my David Hockney original and gave me an hour to get out of London. He said if I didn't I'd end up in more pieces than said mirror."

She raised her eyebrows as he laughed, nervously, remembering that outright terror.

"I'm finished, aren't I?"

Rebecca laughed and patted his head. "Yes," she said. "You are."

THREE

A Kicking In The Street

The copper at the desk hadn't heard of any of them. He stood there with his pen in his hand staring at me like I was something he'd trod in. Fucking copper. If he was any good at his job he'd be out there solving crimes, not standing behind a desk taking notes.

"How many times do I have to tell you? I told your mate the other morning. I gave him all the titles, he's got the list. I get 'em on order from One Stop. Soul stuff, Stevie Wonder, Marvin Gaye, Smokey…"

He wrote down 'soul stuff'.

"That's it? Isn't there nobody you can ask?"

"I'm sorry, sir. It isn't as easy as you'd think. We get burglaries reported all the time. Sometimes we recover everything and sometimes…"

"It's been five fuckin' days now."

"I'll ask you to refrain from using that language, young man, and I won't tell you again."

He nodded over to the bench where some old couple sat holding hands. They looked about a hundred.

This police station stank of disinfectant, reminding me of the early morning shifts I did at Browning's after the cleaners had left. Such crap memories.

"I'm sorry, alright? But I DJ at the Visage on Crown Street…"

"I am familiar with that venue, sir…"

"Every Friday night. I bring me records, they pay me and I get boozed up. Only this Friday I didn't have no records, did I? Cos they got nicked? So until I do get 'em, I'm fired. They won't even let me in as a customer for letting 'em down. They had to replace Soul Nite with sixties stuff at short notice this Friday. You know how many coloureds there are in this town? None of 'em turned up, the till didn't ring and I'm not welcome in there until I get me records back. "

"Is that your only job?"

"It were. I DJ'd four other nights at the place over by the railway arches, smaller place called…"

"Westerton's."

"Only Westy's fired me too. So until you get me records back I'm gonna have to go back to the factory for a crap wage and no free time to score."

"Score?"

"Birds," I said. "Not… the other stuff."

What this copper didn't know was that soon I'd have enough money to sack off working for years.

I could hardly tell him that though, that would've been shafting myself big time. But going back to Browning's, even if it was for another week or two, would kill me. Getting in in the morning, stinking of grease, paint and sweat, crawling into bed and being too knackered to even move before teatime. Nightmare. God knows how the losers there do it for a lifetime.

Fuck that, I was gonna be rich.

"I'll ask around," the copper said. "I'll see what we can do. You seem like a nice lad, Keith. It is Keith?"

I nodded.

"So I'll treat it as a priority. Have you got any Sparks?"

"Have I fuck."

"Watch your mouth."

"Sorry."

"The missus and I may need someone to spin a few tunes on our big day in a few months," he said with a wink.

"Find me fuckin' records then," I said, walking out and saying sorry to the oldies on the bench.

It was roasting outside – had been roasting for days and I'd been spending my afternoons getting a tan. OK, you couldn't see it in the clubs because it was dark, but in daytime I looked the coolest bloke in town, like a white Shaft or someone. I'd been growing my hair too. Being a skinhead looked good and it kept my head cool but I kept getting stopped by the coppers and told to stay out of trouble.

In that burning sun, I walked down the street, seeing some poser in a flowery shirt and big shades going into the Collier's like he wanted everyone to notice him. There was something about my town that attracted pricks.

The telephone box was empty and hadn't been vandalised for a while. There was graffiti inside but nothing that stopped it working.

"Aldo? It's Keith. Keith Moran, you remember?"

Course he remembered me. Aldo the Eyetie was alright. He took all the jokes about them being crap at war well and didn't try to be part of the gang at Browning's. We took the piss out of his accent, mimicking his orders and all that, and he was cool with it. Him and his missus were in Westerton's a few weeks back. Tasty bird – he'd done well there. Yeah, nice bloke Aldo. Knew his place and didn't step out of line.

He was talking at me when I saw the Scimitar go past and pull over in front of the butcher's. Her orange Reliant Scimitar GTE – got looks everywhere it went.

Like her.

She got out and straightened her shades and I watched her with that bold walk go right into the pub, knowing the men in there would turn to get an eyeful. Small world, seeing her like that.

"Aldo, cut to the chase. Have you got anything for me? I got fired from both clubs and need a job. Any shift, I'll even clean the bogs if the money's right."

It took him a few minutes to tell me he was sorry, there was nothing, and I kept having to put money in to keep him on the line. He'd keep his eye out but no, 'sorry Keith, nothing for you right now.'

I hung up then grabbed the receiver and smashed it up and down a few times in one of those moods I had.

No records, no job, nothing doing on the other thing until she said so and then there was this shit with Kelly.

Leaving the receiver dangling and not looking, I opened the door, stepped out and bang!

His fist slammed into my jaw and I went back, smacking my head on the glass, smashing that and sinking to the pavement. It went black for a few moments and I could taste blood in my mouth and then he was blocking out the sunlight, grabbing me by the neck and hauling me to my feet.

"Jim, what the..."

"You know what, you little prick!" he shouted, and threw me across the pavement into the wall.

My head was killing and I slumped to the ground.

I tried to stand up but my legs were too weak. Jim Mudd grabbed my hair, wrenched me up and punched me in the face. Twice. Really hard.

'You don't piss off an old soldier,' he once told me by the fire and he was spot on. He had thirty years and about thirty stone on me.

I think something cracked when I hit the telephone box, hearing it rattle inside.

"Jim, just...," I began, turning with my hands in the air.

The fat bastard aimed a kick at my chest that winded me.

Oh fuck, I was gonna die.

I was gonna die in the street, murdered by my missus's old man, a psycho. A psycho ex-squaddie...

Before sinking to my knees again, I put my hand out to grab hold of something. I reached glass and clutched it. It came away from the frame, a triangle of really sharp glass.

My head pounding, my stomach in knots, I held the glass out towards him, panting. "Come nearer you fat bastard and you'll get this in your cock."

Jim Mudd wiped his bloodied hands on his vest and shook his head.

"I'm serious. Self-defence. I've been in the nick. The copper in there says I'm a nice lad. He'll know I were provoked and you'll be limping for the rest of your days."

Jim Mudd walked towards me, I swung for him but he grabbed my wrist, bent it and headbutted me on the nose. I was falling down when he shoved me into the wall, grabbing me on the rebound and hurling me onto a pile of dustbins where I fell, wondering why weren't there any fucking witnesses? Where were the coppers when you needed them?

One of the dustbins fell over and I went with it, laying back in the rubbish.

Jim Mudd didn't come at me again.

When I opened my right eye, he was kicking broken glass into a grate and rolling his bald head round.

I didn't have the strength to move and ached all over.

"Knitting needles and gin, were it?"

"You what?"

"I said, were it knitting needles and gin?"

"No."

"No, *sir*."

"No, sir. It weren't me that did it."

"It weren't the bleeding Wombles, Keith."

Jim Mudd was leaning on the telephone box and the street was quieter than ever. The Scimitar was still parked. She hadn't seen me get the crap kicked out of me. That was a minor relief.

"There's a doctor Woody told us about. We had to get a train. I paid."

"You little bastard. Not even man enough to do it yourself."

"It could have killed her, sir. I swear I did it that way for her."

"You got rid of the baby then you got rid of Kelly? Or did you get rid of Kelly first?"

"The kid first, sir. I wanted to do the right thing. Kelly's too young. She wants to go to college. She couldn't if she had a kid. If she had a kid she'd be tied to me forever, sir, and I'm going nowhere."

"You can say that again, you little prick."

"I'll never leave this town," I said, spitting out blood and rubbing my ribs. "Kelly will, she'll go far. I wanted what were best for her, sir."

"Why were you in the nick?"

"Eh?"

"You said you've been in the nick."

"I got burgled last week. Scum took all me records. I had the new Stevie Wonder. Were gonna spin it on Friday only they've sacked me. I'm..."

"You're in a real mess, aren't you?"

"Yes, sir. But I'm tough, sir. I'll get by."

Jim Mudd unfolded his arms and shook his head. His fat face softened a bit. "You did it for Kelly?"

I nodded. "We were growing apart, sir. I didn't force her, honest I didn't. Ask her, she'll tell you."

"That's what she said. I wanted to double-check."

"By bouncing me off a telephone box?" I said and wanted to add, *you fucking psycho*.

Jim Mudd spent his youth in trouble, then twenty-five years in the army and now he was just a taxi driver. You paid him to drive you places and he gave you his opinion for nothing, blaming a *bad war* for his temper. Bad war, my backside. He was a nutter, plain and simple.

"You need any money?"

"No, sir.

He looked up to the sky for a few moments then said, "Jesus, Keith. Irene and me could have raised it."

'No you couldn't,' I wanted to say, 'cos what I haven't told you would drive you through the roof.'

The kid wasn't mine.

Its dad was that good-looking waiter at the Star Of India on Derwent Road. Kelly couldn't take her eyes off him when we went for her seventeenth.

2 2

'Do you think he takes the towel off his head when he's getting down to the Wang Dang Doodle?' she wondered.

Well, big Jim Mudd, why don't you ask her?

Why don't you ask your tramp of a daughter whether he was any good when he was poking her in your bed when you were off fishing?

Why don't you ask her why I dumped her?

Why don't you ask Kelly Mudd why she asked me to help her get rid of it instead of seeing your fat red face explode in nine months time?

'Kelly Mudd – so loose you get both your hands inside and start clapping,' was the rumour from the lads at Browning's and I should have listened to it.

Fuck Jim Mudd, I did the right thing. I know it, God knows it and that's all that matters.

But I didn't say any of those things.

I only nodded.

He walked back to where his taxi was parked. "Need a lift anywhere?" he said, rolling down his sleeves and buttoning up his cardigan.

"No."

He opened the door and turned back to me. "Stevie Wonder? Why you listening to that jungle shit? Hey, why does Stevie Wonder smile all the time?"

I shrugged.

"Cos no-one's told him he's coloured," he laughed. "We're marching tomorrow, shag. Marching in *their* streets, on *their* doorsteps. You coming down? The Plough at noon?"

"I'm not a member, sir."

"There's coons in *Crossroads* now, shag. We have to make a stand. You don't need to be a member," Jim

Mudd said. "Just turn up and shout. Maybe get some action afterwards." He got in the car and stuck his fat head out the window. "And shave your bloody hair off."

"I'm growing it," I said. "Like Bowie."

He drove off, giving me a wave.

All that crap – 'making a stand.' What a dickhead. I didn't have a quarrel with nobody. The foreigners walked their side of the street, I walked mine.

The people I did have a quarrel with, apart from him that knocked up my missus, were those who kept telling me what to do and what to think. If it wasn't Jim Mudd wanting me to join the Front or the ginger bird outside British Home Stores insisting I march with Searchlight, it was some other dickhead shoving a leaflet in my hand or getting me to sign something.

'You have to be part of something, be a member of something,' everyone was saying, and all I wanted was to be some*one*. That's all.

And fuck Jim Mudd and his *jungle shit*. He was stuck on Herb Alpert and the Tijuana Brass Band, Acker Bilk and all that crap. Every night I opened with "Soul Limbo" and the coloureds went crazy on that dancefloor, so fuck what he had to say.

As for him who knocked up Kelly, when I could take it no more, I waited for him outside his work at four in the morning with a table leg in my hand. The coppers pinned it on one of the Front seen throwing bottles on a march last May.

That's the way it worked in my town. Dog eat dog. Since I was a kid it was like a kettle on a hob and no way was I gonna be here when it boiled over.

I lay in the rubbish for ten more minutes until my breathing returned to normal and I could stand up.

Stumbling into the barber's a few doors down, I saw Chalky sitting smoking and reading a magazine about David Cassidy.

"You can meet him in Hollywood in this compe... Bloody Hell, Keith," he said. "What happened?"

"I walked into a big *fat* door. Fill that sink up, will you? And get me a towel to wipe this crap off me face."

Chalky flicked the fag on the floor and spent ten minutes helping me get cleaned up, good lad that he is. He gave me his last Wagon Wheel and asked if I'd got my records back before I limped out to where her Scimitar was parked.

I was DJ'ing on a midday till midnight soul session when I first saw her dancing by herself slap bang in the middle of the floor.

And you know what?

She came over to chat me up, looking through my records and telling me what she wanted to hear next. OK, so I'm a pretty boy but it was still a bit odd. Anyway, she was too skinny for me and I was still getting pissed every night over Kelly. Was she pretty? Yeah, but kinda like a bigger sister to me now, only with an arse I could admire.

And here she was, coming out of the gate at the back of the Collier's, not stepping in any of the rubbish that hadn't been taken away for weeks. Oh no, she was too cool for that.

Rebecca Rollins coming along the pavement towards me with the bloke in the poofter's shirt beside her. They weren't touching or anything, they were only walking, but she looked so happy. He was making her smile and he wasn't even trying.

She slowed when she spotted me. They both did.

"Hey Rebecca," I said. "How's it going?"

"What happened to your face?"

"I had an accident."

"You've got stains all over your clothes."

"I fell over. Who's this?"

"Luke Heslin," the bloke said, holding out his hand.

We shook and I got a good look at him. Like a young Robert Redford. That type anyway. Blond, all that.

"Luke, this is Keith Moran. A friend of mine. Keith, Luke's an old schoolfriend who I haven't seen in a few years. Keith DJ's. He's very good, aren't you?"

I couldn't be arsed telling her I'd been robbed, especially with this prick around. "Yeah. Visage and Westerton's."

"Very good," he said. "Perhaps I'll come along one night."

He didn't sound like he meant that.

"Should do," I said. "Get a good crowd in, everyone has a good time."

The bloke nodded and went round the front of the car to the passenger side.

"I'll give you a ring in a couple of days," Rebecca said, climbing into the Scimitar. "We need to catch up."

"Yeah. We do."

"Make sure you get a good wash first," she said, smiling. "You stink."

"Nice to meet you, Keith," the bloke said.

Rebecca pulled out, turned the car round and put her foot down, burning off down the street and screeching round the corner at the end.

I was left standing in the late afternoon sun wondering how much petrol she poured into that thing and where I'd seen that bloke before. It didn't come to me so I shrugged it off and went down to the betting shop, walking through the smoky front and nodding to Booley, who was taking bets off some oldies.

Out the back sat my pride and joy, the Ducati 450 Desmo, all sexy in scarlet. Booley let me leave it in his yard whenever I needed to and he never asked for money or anything like that.

Starting her up, I pulled out the gate and roared off down the alley, kids scattering as I flew by with no helmet, no leathers, no nothing.

I turned right, crossed Wroughton Street and headed straight over to get out of town and onto Tallentyre Way, getting some right speed up by the time I reached the Plough on the corner.

After that kicking, I needed some Keith Moran time. Some freedom. An escape from everything. This bike was the only thing that could take me out of my crap life.

After the Labour Exchange, I really let her go, heading out towards the cooling towers in the distance.

I was thinking, maybe pick up some ale and have a drink by the canal in the sun?

Five minutes from the bookies and I was out of town and Jim Mudd was out of my head. Glorious. Head out on the highway and all that.

Only that's when they got me.

Sirens behind, one of theirs, pulling out from the trading estate, coming right up the road. It overtook, the driver signalling me to slow down.

I sidled into a verge and sat there as they parked up, got out and came back to me, shaking their heads parrot fashion.

"Engine off, please, fella," one said. "Now tell me why we've stopped you."

"Too fast?"

"For starters. Secondly: no helmet. What if you fell off?"

"I'd die."

"You would. Your skull'd cave in and your *hair* wouldn't be the same again, would it?"

"No, constable. Thank you for bringing it to me attention."

"Do you have a helmet?"

"It were stolen, constable. I reported it."

"Quite. As you said, you were going too fast. You were riding like a guilty man. Like this motorcycle doesn't belong to you."

"Oh, it's definitely mine, constable. I bought it with money from me mam's will. I've had it two years."

"In that case, you'll have a licence. Let me see it."

"I don't carry it with me, constable. I... I do have one but I don't carry it with me."

He scowled. "What good is that, fella? What if you had to produce it? Like now?"

"I'm sorry, constable. I'll keep it with me from now on, I promise."

"Where are you from?"

I told him.

"Now that *is* unfortunate," he said. "Because Waddicor and I aren't local bobbies. So tomorrow morning you're gonna have quite a ride ahead of you to bring a copy of your licence to our nick."

"What nick would that be, constable?"

"Stanley Street."

"Stanley Street? Where's that?"

He told me with a massive smile on his face, the smug bastard. Fucking Hell, it was thirty miles away. I couldn't afford the petrol for that. Fuck these clowns. If they wanted to see my licence, they could find me.

"Name?"

"Keith Moran."

"Eleven o'clock, tomorrow morning, fella," he said, walking back to the panda. "And make sure you've got a helmet on."

I looked at the other one, Waddicor, looking sympathetic at me. "Why you over here?"

"Carrying out cycling proficiency tests at your Civic Centre," he said. "For the young 'uns. Your local bobbies are too busy to carry them out."

"Really?" I said, thinking of the copper who wanted Sparks playing at his wedding and thinking how no-one had seen the kicking I'd taken. "Doing fuckin' *what* exactly?"

FOUR

Mr. Browning

"Have a look in there," she said. "See what you can find."

"Shouldn't you be concentrating on the road? And on not getting pulled over?"

Christ, she drove fast but it suited her. Bare arms and white driving gloves was a strange combination but she carried it off.

He rummaged in the glove compartment as they swerved round another corner passing the steelworkers finishing – each and every one of them turning to stare.

"*A Nod's As Good As A Wink...* It's a bit old. Will that do?"

"Put it on. And wind down your window. It's August and we're having fun."

Heslin stuck the tape in the deck and leaned back in his seat, unable to believe how things had changed today.

"They're my favourite band," she was saying. "Rod's my ideal man. I think it's the voice."

He nodded, watching the ironworks come and go, then the gasworks and the immigrant side of town. Soon they were out in the country, The Faces blasting out of the tape deck, the sun blazing down, and the sexy bitch next to him singing about "Miss Judy's Farm".

"And the hair as well. I love his hair. I've seen them a couple of times. He's all presence on stage. Have you ever thought about growing your hair?"

"Only if the role required it."

"What music do you listen to?"

"Everything. I like a bit of everything. Sparks can piss off though."

She smiled at him. A big wide smile.

They sped on, climbing into the hills now until suddenly she braked hard and the car slid into a space beside the road. Rebecca turned the tape off, got out and walked round to his side.

"You see that?" she said. "You know what it is?"

Heslin shifted in his seat and looked down into the valley at the huge red brick building beneath the three chimneys reaching into the sky. A small straight road led right into the complex, a ditch on either side. Round the building ran a high brick wall.

He'd seen it before. Everyone from round here had.

"Lyons' Paint Factory," he said.

"Not Lyons' anymore. He sold up and it became Browning's three years ago. Now Browning wants to sell the land to clear his debts. The local papers reckon he'll get hundreds of thousands and they'll build a housing estate there. It'd have its own bus route."

"What's this got to do with Rod Stewart?"

"Nothing," she said, smiling sweetly. "I just wondered if you knew about anything that's gone on since you deserted us."

She came round and got back in.

"I shut this place out when I left," he murmured. "I didn't have too many happy memories of it. Craphouse. All chimneys, factories and rundown boozers. Even in August it oozes shit. God definitely made it on a wet Sunday."

"You're a snob."

"I'm not. I just didn't wanna grow old in a place that stifles you. All the ambitious people leave."

She stared at him for a few moments, her hands on the steering wheel. It unnerved him a bit. She seemed to be studying him or sizing him up.

"Do your parents live here?"

"She died giving birth to me. He sodded off to Scotland with his new old lady a few years back."

"Any brothers or sisters?"

"None that I know of. Why all the questions? I don't know anything about you yet."

"We'll chat at my house, I told you."

"And where is yours?"

"You'll find out soon. Now, 'Clunk click, every trip.'"

She pressed play, put it in gear and roared off, handbraking it after a hundred yards or so. The Scimitar spun one-eighty, sending gravel flying.

Rebecca paused a few moments, letting the engine purr, then whispered, "It's back this way."

It was a part of town he'd never been to before.

He didn't even know there were houses here. He almost caught the name of the street, something-Balk Lane, as she sped past, and a mile or so down the road, she pulled into the driveway of a semi. Nineteen-thirties, he guessed.

"Here," she said, handing him keys. "Open the garage."

Heslin climbed out and hurried to the large white wooden doors, pulling them open and standing back to let her pull in. The garden stretched back quite far and was flanked by trees either side. At the end sat a smashed up greenhouse and a rusting lawnmower. In front of that, a large pond.

Turning round, he got a good look at the house. Two storeys, maybe an attic, and a sun lounge full of plants by the kitchen at this end. The sun lounge didn't match the rest of the place. It was too modern. Whoever owned this place had money, that was certain.

"The quietest street in town," Rebecca said, closing the door. "No neighbours."

"Why not?"

She shrugged. "Who knows? But at least it means we don't have to keep the noise down."

"Whose is it?"

"My boyfriend's."

"Eh?"

She stepped into the kitchen and he followed her in, clocking the classy green floral wallpaper and red lino flooring.

Rebecca put her bag on the side. "There's wine in the cabinet in there," she said. "The glasses are in the cupboard. You pour, I'm going to change."

He watched her walk down the hallway and heard her pad upstairs before he stuck his head round a door into the back room and got a look at the sun lounge. Rammed with orchids and cactus plants, two wicker chairs, a wicker divan, small telly, record player and standard lamp. Heslin went over to the cabinet and took out a bottle of red, seeing all the other booze in there. Black Label, Advocaat, Cinzano, all that stuff. If she liked drinking as much as he did, they were in for a great night.

"Not that I'm a prude or anything," he called. "But won't your boyfriend have something to say about you bringing another man back?"

"I doubt it," she said, her voice sounding muffled.

"In the navy, is he?"

"No," he heard her call as he moved the bottles around. "He's dead."

"Shit. That's… rubbish. I didn't know," he said.

"How would you? We've only just met."

Yeah, he thought, I need to keep telling myself that.

There was a litre of Smirnoff in there, already open. He unscrewed the top and took a big shot. It wasn't Dutch courage exactly, more like a relaxant. It got him through auditions and screwing a bird for the first time was always a kind of audition. If you weren't any good – and he always was – they didn't call you back.

Heslin smiled at his analogy and went back into the kitchen.

Rebecca appeared in a green robe, her hair tied up but her arms not bare anymore. "Haven't you opened it yet? Go through and relax."

In the back room, he tucked his legs under him on the chair, looking out through the sun lounge, hearing her moving round the kitchen. For a few moments, he was tempted to have another shot.

It was a relief when she brought the whole bottle in with their drinks. That was a good sign. Wine was harder to quit than ale when he got started. It was what wooftas drank, yeah, but it was so moreish and got him feeling better than the other stuff. Plus there was less liquid so he didn't have to water the horse as much. It'd be years before he drank it in pubs though. She'd have to be someone really special to get him to order a bottle of Mateus Rose in a dump like the Collier's Arms.

"So?"

"So... what?"

"Here we are," he said. "Rebecca Rollins, girl from college, flash car, takes me on a geography field trip, tells me I'm a snob and now we're back at the house owned by... Sorry."

"You can say it," she said, sipping. "My dead boyfriend."

This was a new scenario and he didn't have a bloody clue what to say to that. His policeman in *Motown Cop* would have handled it fine, he thought, but best to not get too attached to him, yeah?

"So how did it come about with Sidney King?" she said, setting her wine down on a small table.

"Do we have to talk about that?"

"I want to know what brings a famous movie star into my house."

He sighed. "I was pissed off at him, I suppose. And pissed too. Not a great combination."

"Why pissed off?"

"I suppose," he said, and stopped. "Because I turned down a career in pornography to get where I am. Hardcore stuff they shoot in Doncaster. I turned that down because I wanted to be a serious actor with a body of work I was proud of and I struggled and struggled to get recognition. Then on the last day of shooting he called me over, saying he wanted me to meet a couple of friends of his. I recognised them from the papers and thought, no way am I shaking their hands. All it takes is one photo and my career's up in smoke, closed set or no closed set, yeah? Apparently they could do me all sorts of favours, make me a bigger star than I thought was possible. Speaking to me like that? Piss off. I don't need favours from scum like them just for a few more lines on camera."

"You have a lovely way with words."

Heslin rubbed his eyes before he spoke again. "I told them right out, I didn't want anything from them and they were having nothing from me. I walked away."

"You hoped that would be the end of it?"

"*Hoped*, yeah. Sid turned up to my dressing room later, furious. He threw Estes out and started ranting. I told him it was nothing personal and he seemed to calm down."

Rebecca lay back on her moquette and crossed her legs. He had a glance but couldn't see whether or not she had anything on underneath.

"Why didn't you leave it there?"

"Oh, it gets worse. My agent called me up and told me none too-subtly that Mr. King wasn't a man to cross. Implying…"

She nodded, slowly.

"Look," Heslin said. "If I climbed to the top the right way, I'm staying on top the right way."

"Very noble."

"After I blabbed, my doorbell rang nonstop. Not from Sid or his friends but more journos. The two bastards who woke me on Thursday morning didn't bother with the doorbell and shoved over my plant on their way out. So I got the first train up here," Heslin said, finishing his wine. "To hide out."

"Where are you staying?"

"Mrs. Swallow's."

"And what's she like?"

"Looks more like a spitter."

"Oh Luke, don't be vulgar."

"Alright," he said, his attempt at humour having failed. "She's very old, very ugly with thick glasses. It's tinned ravioli for tea, Rice Krispies for breakfast and she always has the top of the milk."

"Anything else?"

"Naked bulb and a crusty smell in the hallway, the wallpaper's peeling and the springs are coming through my bed. I notice things by the way. What else? Oh yeah, above my bed there's an embroidered quote in a frame."

"Saying?"

"'Buy More British Eggs.'"

Rebecca smiled at him. A fond smile, enjoying his company. "Did you bring a change of clothes? Not that brown cords don't suit you," she said, raising her eyebrows slightly.

"Course I have. Anyway, what's that called? Your robe?"

"A kimono. You like it?"

"Less is more for me."

"Is that the line famous movie stars use?"

"How would I know?"

He poured them both more wine and sat beside her on the moquette, casually to make it look unplanned.

"As a man in hiding, you can stay here," she said. "Bring your things over tomorrow. Rent-free but you'd have to help me out with a few jobs."

Oh Jesus, don't say she just wanted to be friends.

"But if this gets out, you'll be…"

"Trust me, no reporters could ever find you here. No-one ever calls by."

"Really?"

"No-one. No War On Want, no Scouts wanting to wash your car, no Jehovah's Witnesses. It's a ghost street, honestly."

"Sounds fine. Thank you. Don't take this the wrong way but what do you do? For a job? Do you work?"

She shook her head. "I'll go back one day or find something I like. Running a café abroad would be nice."

"But if you don't work, how...?"

"Fred keeps me."

"Fred?"

"My boyfriend. He left me quite a bit, including this place. I don't want to be here much longer, I'm going to sell up in a few months when the recession's ended and people stop striking long enough to buy it."

Heslin looked hard at her and vowed not to answer any more of her questions until she'd told him more. It never normally happened like this. She wanted to do more of the talking stuff before the sex and he was used to being naked on the floor within five minutes of meeting a fan. But if she wanted to take it slow, so could he. She looked worth it.

"What happened to him?"

"Why do you want to...?"

"You know all about me. It's your turn."

"I know all about you because you're only too happy to keep on about yourself," she snapped.

"Hey, I was... Alright, I'm sorry. I'm just..."

"He was run over. Five months ago. March fifteenth."

"Bloody Hell."

Rebecca necked the rest of her wine and poured herself more. "He was coming home from a gig one night, separated from his friends. Only a few streets away and a drunk hit him. Fred went up the bonnet and died in the road. It was my fault really," she said softly. "I should have picked him up."

"Jesus, that's really shit," he said, wishing for a more polite way to describe it.

"Yes," she said. "And like your story, it gets worse."

"How could it get worse?"

"Everyone knows who did it. He drove off but they found him a few days later, Fred's blood on his car. Blood on his hands. Yet he walked."

"How?"

"It didn't even come to court. They hushed it up because it was embarrassing. Two policemen visited and said it was in the interests of the town that they fitted someone else up for it."

"I don't get this at all."

"They pinned a manslaughter charge on a child molester who had got away with some nasty business in the past. They used my Fred's death as an excuse to nail a pervert and expected me to think that was alright. Get the vodka, Luke."

"Where is it?"

"You know where it is," she said. "You've got the look of someone who searches for booze in every building he enters. I imagine you knock it back like Kia-Ora."

Jesus, she really did have his number.

Shaking his head, Heslin got up and went into the kitchen, getting out tall glasses from a cupboard. He came back, dug out the Smirnoff from the back of the cabinet and poured them a large measure each.

"It would kill Mr. Browning's political aspirations, was what they said."

"Browning? As in…"

"Norman Browning, from the factory."

"Is that why you showed me that? Hang on, Rebecca. This is all moving a bit fast for me. Not that I don't like fast, yeah, but it's going fast in a strange direction. Why are you telling me all this?"

She was smiling softly at him. "I want your help."

"Help?"

"That's right."

"You'll have to spell it out to me."

"That boy we met this afternoon – Keith? He's agreed already. We only need another pair of hands. Justice for Fred," she murmured. "You're perfect. You're just what I need."

He wanted to walk out, really he did, but the only thing he wanted more than that was to hear her out and it was starting to seem like that screw was on the cards.

Stay right where you are, Luke, he told himself silently, it's a bloody long walk back to that cow's boarding house.

"I never even met Fred, why do I wanna…?"

"Because you'll get rich in the process. Surely that's incentive enough for a man whose career is in freefall?"

"Don't say that," he said sharply.

Rebecca laughed lightly and leant in to give him a peck on the cheek. He turned to make his move, closing in on her mouth but she pulled back.

"OK Luke," she said, clamping her hand across his lips. "Let's forget it for now. Let's have a few more drinks and relax. Then you can sleep on it. But something tells me tomorrow you'll be more than willing to help us out."

FIVE

The Plough

Woody got sent down for selling weed out of his uncle's ice cream van, telling me when I went to visit him I could watch his place until he got out.

No arguments here – he had the coolest gaff in town.

The nineteen thirteen Picture Palace on Duke Street was where he had his rooms, right at the top where they used to store the film reels. I didn't know how he'd got it but the rent was paid up till January and it had everything I could want – sink, bed, colour telly from Rumbelows, cupboards, a wardrobe and somewhere to make food. Not only that but before they'd been nicked, I could play my records as loud as I wanted without neighbours getting pissed off.

Woody left me the key to the roof as well so I could go up there and get a view of the town, spying on the birds below and all that.

I was up there when I saw her Scimitar pull into the street and park up.

She got out – all in brown with white driving gloves – and came in through the door. I ran down the stairs and checked myself out in the mirror. Still battered and bruised thanks to that bastard.

I was looking through my drawers for my licence when she walked straight in – she never knocked – and sat down.

"I got you this," I said, throwing her a copy of *Vogue*. "Peter Sellers interviews Michael Caine."

"'There's A Change In Fashion'," she read off the cover. "That's very sweet of you, Keith. Spending forty pence on me."

"Give over. I looked like a right girl buying that. Him behind the counter probably thought I were queer or something."

She flicked through it as I went and closed the door. When I turned round she was holding up *Buster and Cor!!*, her eyebrows raised.

"So what?" I said. "They're easy reading."

"You're twenty-two, Keith," she said, like she was telling me off. "Maybe it's time to start on the classics."

"I read *Skinhead* a few months back. Anyway, where's that bloke?"

"Who?" she said, leaning down to brush something from her foot.

"That ponce I saw you with yesterday."

Crossing her legs and dropping the magazine on the floor, she gave me one of her smiles. "He's right where I want him," she said. "And he's going nowhere."

"You what?"

"Let's just say he's relaxing in the sun."

I sat on the bed. "What's going on? Who is he?"

"He was a movie star. From round here originally."

"Called?"

"Luke Heslin. Did you see *Motown Cop* on the television last month?"

"Oh crap, that were him."

"That's him."

"I knew I recognised him from somewhere. That were good, that. Wow. I've not met anyone famous before."

"Then you're in luck."

"Why?

"Because he's coming in with us."

"What? Why?"

"Because…"

"We don't need nobody else!"

"Listen to me, Keith."

"It's just me and you now Woody's gone, you said. We've done all the work. We don't want him coming in with us, taking our winnings."

"We need someone else."

"We don't! Please Rebecca. There'll be less for us if he joins us. Get rid of him. I can do it myself."

She shook her head.

"What good's an actor gonna do anyway? What did you tell him?"

She stood up and went over to the window, leaning out and giving me a great view of her arse. "I told him about Fred."

"And Browning?"

"That too."

"Is he in on it?"

"He was reluctant at first but I've talked him round," she said.

"What does that mean? You danced on his lance?"

"Keith…"

"What do you mean?"

"Never you mind." She sat back down, crossing her legs again. "Have you got the floor plan of Browning's yet?"

"Yeah. Aldo got me one a few days ago. He doesn't know why. Probably doesn't care."

"Was he suspicious?"

"Aldo? Nah, he's just glad to help out. Get this though – I might have to go back to work there unless we do it soon."

"Why?

"Me records got nicked, didn't they? I got fired from the Visage and Westerton's. I need money so I rang Aldo but he's got nowt for me."

"You'll have money soon," she said. "Don't worry."

"I'm not worried, I just wanna get going. Look, could you lend me some so I can fill up me bike? Take it out of my share."

She reached into her bag, took out her purse and dug out some pound notes, coming over to me. I took them and she stood there, tidying my hair up for a few seconds while she spoke. "Keep the money," she said. "About Luke... You've no need to worry, he'll be fine. It'll make it easier, two rather than one."

"I suppose," I said, but wasn't coming round to it.

I didn't like the idea of sharing her with some actor or anyone for that matter. *Motown Cop* had been great though. Me and Jim Mudd watched it with some cans while Kelly and her mam were out at the ice rink. I could still hear Jim Mudd saying he bet it cost a fortune when the S-type ploughed into the river at the end. He hated the coloured bloke though, surprise surprise.

"I'll bring him over one afternoon," she said, finishing with my hair, "so you can be properly introduced. We'll go over the plan."

"It won't take long. I know Browning's place like the back of me hand. And I know what route they patrol at night. All that kinda crap. We need to do it on a Saturday when the nightshift isn't on. There'll only be Cheesey and Terry in then and we can avoid 'em easy."

Rebecca folded her arms, flexing her fingers and looked at me, all thoughtful. "Good boy."

"All this?" I said. "This factory business? I were thinking last night, aren't there other ways of getting your own back?"

"Such as?"

"I don't know but…"

"The way to break a man's heart is through his wallet, Keith. Remember that."

"I suppose. Don't forget *Vogue*," I said pointing to it on the floor.

"You keep it. I don't like Sellers." She put her bag on her shoulder, flicking her hair softly and putting her shades on. "Look, I should be going. I have an actor who's itching for me to get back to him," she said, tickling under my chin. "Literally."

Just like that, she thought it was gonna be OK.

She wanted this actor to come in with us and thought it was that simple. Don't get me wrong, I'm all for teamwork – I was a centre forward until I did my back in – and at Browning's, me and the lads were always chipping in to help each other out.

But this wasn't anything like that.

Me and Rebecca had worked out this scheme together. She'd done all the reading about Norman Browning – gone through all the papers, listened to all the gossip about him. She'd even parked up on the hill with a pair of binos watching us all striking a few months back.

It was such a good scheme, especially for a woman. I sometimes couldn't believe that it was a woman who'd thought it all up. We didn't need an actor jumping in with us but if she wanted him, well, I could hardly walk away now, could I?

I was going down the stairs to get my bike when I ran into Jim Mudd coming up. "Alright shag?" he said like we were best mates. "Coming to join us? You said you would."

"I said I might but..."

"Come on then."

"I'm not a member."

"You don't need to be a member."

"I'm not..."

Being on narrow stairs made this even more awkward. The fat bastard was glaring up at me and for a moment I thought he might charge me.

"What's up with you these days?"

"Eh?"

"You've become such a little..."

"What?"

"A poof, Keith. You're so soft. I don't even know you anymore."

I bit my lip for the second time in as many days wanting to tell him everything I knew.

Jim Mudd learning how I was gonna hit the big time in a matter of days, walking away with some Tory bastard's money in my pocket for an hour's work or so. Yeah, really fucking soft.

"I told the lads you'd come down."

"What lads? I don't know any of 'em."

"Dobbo, you know Dobbo?"

"No. Look, Jim, I've got to fill up me bike...?"

"Well, come for a pint after then? The Plough at threeish?"

"Alright," I sighed. "But don't call me soft again, OK? That beating I took yesterday, that weren't how a fairy takes things, were it?"

Jim Mudd smiled and shook his head. "Dobbo couldn't believe it when I told him you were gonna slice me. He says 'Get him down here, we'll give him someone to slice up good and proper.'" Jim Mudd turned and went down the stairs and I followed. "See you at three," he said. "Don't back out."

I crossed the road to the lock-up, getting my bike out and roaring off. No helmet, no leathers, none of that crap.

It was three on the dot when I went into the smoky Plough, being spotted by a pissed-up Jim Mudd straight away.

If ever there was a pub I shouldn't have been in, it was here. Beer mats plastered to the walls, smashed dartboard and two boarded up windows. It was a little boy's idea of a man's pub, hardly a fucking Berni Inn.

The place was heaving with skinheads of all ages and the staff were struggling to cope. I shoved through to where Jim Mudd was standing and he put his arm around me, introducing me to all his mates with their crap nicknames.

"This little sod sacked off coming with us," Jim Mudd was saying and his audience shook their heads.

I kept schtum and drank silently.

"Your mam got you running errands, has she?" the one called Dobbo said.

"Leave it, Dobbo, he's…"

47

"Me mam's dead, you wanker. So don't go..."

"Jesus, I didn't..."

"Come on, Keith. He didn't know. Dobbo, say sorry."

"I'm sorry, mate. I wouldn't have said anything if I'd known. You a member?"

"No."

"You should join. It's more a social club than anything, eh Jim?"

"Yeah, but we take it seriously. It's..."

I felt someone bang into my back and I turned to see some bloke, bit older than me carrying four pint pots. A real hard case, tattoos of spiders on his neck and all. "Watch it, dickhead," he said. "I coulda fuckin' spilt these then."

"You walked into me," I said quietly.

"I *will* fuckin' walk into you, sunshine, you get in my way again. Do you know who I am?"

"No."

"I'm Stake's brother. Alright?"

Jim Mudd didn't speak up for me this time. Dobbo looked at his shoes and the others couldn't have cared less.

I nodded, thinking, what's your name then, Kidney? He glared at me, made a comment about my hair and walked off.

The pub got louder and louder, someone started chanting and soon it was my round.

I shoved past skinheads and ended up at the bar, ringing the bell for service. I spotted Kidney or whatever his name was next to me, bragging to his pals about some twins he'd boned. It took ages for the barmaid to serve me – long enough for me to hear Kidney start on about the Chinky on Gillis Street, Hing Lung's was it?

"Come on," he was saying. "It's a laugh. Shit him right up."

"And do what?" one of his pals said.

Kidney shrugged. "I don't know. We haven't had a tear-up in months, have we? Break his fingers, screw his daughters. In and out before he even has chance to call his Triads up. Trash the place. Get fed while we're there."

"We're robbin' him?"

Kidney grabbed his pal's cheeks and looked him straight in the eyes, saying, "No, Dewey. We're *learnin'* him. Got it?"

His mates were nodding, really up for it.

See, this is what I meant about being part of something. You have to follow someone and do what they do, and like what they like, and before you know it your independence is out the window and you're right up someone's arse.

I liked Bogart saying, 'I stick my neck out for no fucker.' He was right on the money. Look out for yourself and no-one else.

"Get there for six," Kidney said. "All of us. And we'll show 'em."

Although – and maybe this was the beer thinking – sometimes you *could* look out for others without straying from yourself too much...

Kidney turned, seeing me and staring. I paid for the four pints and then he was in my face, his temple touching mine. "Alright dickhead?" he said. "Know who I am yet?"

"Stake's brother."

"You think you're funny?"

"That's what you said."

"You have that and get out of my drinker, alright? Don't you ever drink in my boozer again, long-haired poof. You're still here in five minutes, me, I'm throwing you through that window, alright?"

Jim Mudd was looking over, all worried. I hadn't eaten all day and the three pints had gone to my head making me tipsy enough to be brave. I nodded and walked away.

This job at Browning's better go off big time, I thought, the week I'm having.

I didn't join in with Jim Mudd and his mates slating Wilson and his immigration policy. I finished my pint and went back to the bar, ordering a pint of Special. She served me straight away this time. I let her keep the change, took a deep breath and went over to the skinheads.

"Excuse me," I said, interrupting Kidney doing an impression of Dickie Davies.

"You again, you f...," he began.

"Here," I said. "This is for you."

"You... what?"

"To say sorry."

"Sorry?"

"Yeah. Sorry."

"Are you...? Dickhead."

I stared him down, he didn't know what to say and his mates kept still too. He could hardly throw me through the window for buying him a pint, could he? After a long glare, he took it and told me to fuck off.

I turned and left them to it, saying bye to Jim Mudd and checking my watch on my way out.

Five twenty-one.

I had thirty-nine minutes.

Shit.

I ran across the road and through the railway arches, turning right onto the rec and running across there as fast as my pissed-up legs let me.

Reaching the gates, it was five twenty-nine.

Thirty-one minutes.

I had to wait for a train at the crossing, getting my breath back for a bit. I missed a bus by two seconds and some kids asked if I wanted to buy a lathe when I cut over the school fields.

It was five fifty-two when I got to the lock-up, getting out my bike and roaring off to Gillis Street, making it in four minutes.

Hing Lung's opened at half five. I knew because I'd been in loads of times with Kelly.

Leaving the bike on the pavement, I went in and the bloke recognised me straight away. "Hallo, my fren," he said, with a grin.

"Get out," I said. "Get out and lock up for the night."

He frowned and his two daughters in the back looked up at me. God, this was gonna get me in Intensive Care if Kidney and co. found me here.

"There's men on their way here. They're gonna vandalise the place. Do you understand? You're gonna get destroyed if you don't lock up."

He didn't get it at all.

"You two, you speak English? Come here. You saw the skinheads marching today?"

They nodded.

"Right. Tell daddy that them skinheads are on their way here right now and they are going to *Beat. Him. Up* unless he locks up for the night. OK?"

One nodded, frightened. The other spoke to her old man quickly and he started running round like a madman.

The clock said five fifty-nine.

At one minute past six, the shutters were down and I was in a telephone box down the street, calling the coppers.

Kidney and his mates came round the corner a few minutes later, Kidney's mates laughing at him for picking the one day the Chinky was closed.

He started booting the shutters and, from where I stood, I could see the sisters looking out from an unlit window upstairs. The gang started shouting the usual crap, kicking and punching defenceless corrugated metal and were still at it when two panda cars screeched round the corner and onto the pavement, trapping them between them.

I smiled as coppers piled out, one big bastard landing a punch squarely on Kidney's chin and another couple in his ribs.

It had turned into a free for all when I walked up, skinheads being bounced off car bonnets, Kidney being handcuffed and booted in the groin. I had to stop and watch as they were shoved in the back and driven off, Kidney's bleeding eyes opening wide when he saw me.

Two coppers stayed behind to speak to Mr. Hing Lung and waiting for him to come down, they spotted me. "Are you part of this?"

"No."

"You sure?"

"Come on Ernie," the other one said. "Does he look like one of 'em? Look at his hair."

"I'm growing it," I said, walking back to where I'd left my bike. "Like Bowie."

Good deed for the day, that.

Anyway, about that pint I bought old Kidney stone?

That was to say sorry for what I was about to do. I got him it by way of apology for fucking with his evening's entertainment. He still doesn't know that. Never will. To this day, that pint's probably still frying his tiny mind. But fuck that skinhead. Nobody tells me where I can and can't drink no matter what they've got tattooed on their neck.

SIX

Roadside Picnic

It took ten minutes to pack his suitcase at Mrs. Swallow's and then he was straight on the telephone in the hallway to Melanie.

"It's a clear message, Mel," Heslin said, scratching at his burnt chest. "I want you to make sure Sid knows I'm truly sorry. Yeah? Tell him I won't ever feel as bad about anything as I do about this. Sid's the only man in the world to take me under his wing like he did and I hate myself for being so bloody foolish. And ungrateful, mention that, yeah? How's it looking?"

She sighed. "Not good."

"Not good? How?"

"Sid had a meeting with Dean yesterday. I don't think Dean can get you out of this one."

"What does that mean?"

"Ring me later. I'll see what I can find out."

"Tell him I'm sorry, Mel, tell him…"

The line clicked dead.

Heslin stood there, head against the wall, hearing the ticking clock above him. That sinking feeling again.

"Mr. Heslin?" That cow, coming in from the kitchen. "Can I ask that you keep your shirt buttoned at all

times? I run a respectable establishment and I don't
encourage nakedness among my guests. And we agreed
upon the curfew for ten. I sat up until ten-thirty for the
past two nights waiting for you. It will not do."

"I got sunburnt yesterday," he said, pointing to his
chest. "I'm not a guest anymore. And I've been with a
lady since Monday. So ask what you like but you won't
get it."

He punched the telephone and went out the front
with his suitcase, heading right for the Collier's Arms
and that first pint.

Heslin had a couple out the back, calming down at last
and starting to think clearly.

His chest still stung like mad and it was a lobster red
colour, even after he'd used a whole bottle of calamine
on it. Last night he'd rolled onto his front in his sleep and
woken in agony.

Bitch.

Finishing his dregs, he took the glass back to the bar.
"That woman who was in here on Monday?" he said to
the barman. "Do you know her?"

"What woman?"

"She was sitting out there. Brown hair, bare arms?"

"I didn't see her, chief," he said and continued
polishing his glasses. "Fancy a coffee? And a roll?"

"I don't... I don't understand."

"Branching out, chief," the barman said with a wink.
"Branching out."

Heslin went to water the horse then out into the
street, walking past the record shop, hearing Clapton
asking the Lord to give him the strength to carry on,
and almost smiling. He crossed the road, heading to

the park and was near the gates when he heard that familiar roar.

"Ready?" she called out, leaning over to open his door.

He shrugged and climbed in, Rebecca putting her foot down as he got his belt on.

"How's your chest?"

"It kills, how did you think it'd be?"

"Sorry," she smiled.

"How's your eye?"

"It'll heal. I put more eyeshadow on this morning and these," – she touched her shades – "they'll cover it."

They drove in silence for a few minutes until she asked if he liked her hair in pigtails. He said no, it didn't suit her, made her look like a child. She thanked him.

It was awkward. Not quite as awkward as yesterday but there was still that atmosphere.

She headed north out of town, getting onto the deserted main road and flooring it as they climbed into the hills on the same road from two days ago. They stopped in the same place and turned to look down at Browning's place.

"I made us a picnic," she said. "There's a couple of bottles for you in there too."

"Oh."

"But from your mood, I'm guessing you've had a drink already."

"Why do you care?"

"Oh Luke, aren't we friends anymore?"

He turned to face her, not knowing whether he hated her or adored her as she raised her eyebrows and turned her lips down, pouting for effect.

"I don't wanna be a part of this, alright?"

"But you already are. And you know why you can't drop out."

Heslin shook his head.

He got out and stood at the side of the road watching the throng of strikers outside the factory gates. They held placards and banners, shouting stuff he couldn't hear. The Union Rep stood on a car bonnet with a loud hailer and, again, the words didn't carry this high but the sound did.

There were police at one end of the line. Yeah, itching to get their hands dirty. They'd probably have chance when Browning rolled in.

Up here it was silent. Not a breath of wind and no sound from her in the car.

If she'd thrown his suitcase out and driven off now, he'd feel better. That'd be half of his problems solved. Sod it, she could drive off with his suitcase. He didn't give a damn so long as she did drive off.

He went back and leant in. "Beer."

She reached into the hamper and handed one over.

He opened it with the key to his London flat. "What does Browning drive?"

"A TR6," she said, leaning back in her seat. "Navy blue."

He took a big swig, leaning on the Scimitar, gazing at the three chimneys not giving out anything today. "Yesterday," he said. "I thought you said you didn't fancy me?"

"I imagined you were someone else."

"I thought you might."

"Rod," she sighed.

He took another drink. "You're a bitch, do you know that?"

She laughed. "You'll thank me when you're rich, you know you will. We need you."

"You've got a ridiculous way of auditioning people."

"It worked, didn't it?"

"Piss off."

"How did it make you feel?"

"What?"

"Yesterday. How did it make you feel?"

"Which part? The first or the second?"

Rebecca laughed. "Never mind, don't answer. I know how you felt. Poor Luke."

"Piss off," he spat and walked away.

A few minutes later he saw the navy Triumph appear at the end of the road below and head towards the factory. It stopped at a line of policemen who crowded round.

"He's here."

Rebecca got out of the car with the binoculars and hurried over, raising her shades and looking through them at the action below. "They're probably telling him to turn back today," she said. "And he's probably saying 'Do you know who I am?' What do you think? Hey, did you ever use that line?"

Heslin kept quiet, drinking more as the line opened and the Triumph sped up towards the gates. A roar came from somewhere and everyone broke ranks, rushing at the vehicle which wasn't slowing. Heslin saw the Union Rep shouting at them – the gist being to calm down and listen to him? – through the loud hailer.

Men banged on the car windows and on the bonnet, trying to climb on the roof and falling by the wayside. The police moved in, swinging truncheons at the strikers and soon an almighty ruck had broken out.

Browning ploughed on as strikers started dropping policemen and policemen started booting strikers on the ground. Blows were rained down everywhere – the noise getting louder as policemen from the first line charged up towards the factory, bringing reinforcements to their men.

The Union Rep climbed onto the roof of his car and began to scream into the loud hailer, urging everyone to remain calm.

A man in green overalls jumped onto the bonnet of the Triumph and fell clumsily, rolling down into the ditch as the car finally reached the gates, now swinging open.

"He should have been more careful," Heslin muttered. "He could have ended up like Fred."

That should have got a reaction from her, should have got her blood up and made her start hissing. He wanted it to, wanting to hurt her with cruel words. But she didn't say or do anything, other than stare at the carnage below before handing the binos over.

Browning got out of his car and Heslin finally got a good look at the bastard.

Thick black hair, fake tan and tailored navy suit. Probably had cufflinks on his shirt too and got his shoes shined every morning, the bleeding Triumph driver. He was straightening his collar, looking at his employees at the gate before he turned and went into his factory.

"He's making a point," Heslin said. "He doesn't need to be in today. If he did, he'd have got in sooner."

Heslin watched the ruck continue, seeing the Union Rep being helped from the roof of his car as the violence escalated. "It's like the bloody animal kingdom."

"Come on," Rebecca said, taking him by the elbow. "Let's eat."

She spread out a blanket on the ground behind him as he watched the factory, going from window to window with the binos.

Heslin didn't know why but he lingered on the far right corner of the building. He spied a door built into the top floor that opened out onto what must have been an eighty foot drop onto a glass roof. There was a gap of five feet between that and a solitary smokestack. Yeah, he didn't know why but he studied that part of the building for longer than any other.

"Minor criminal blip over forever," he muttered, lowering the binos.

"Pardon?"

"Nothing," he said. "A line from *Motown Cop* came to me. I don't know why."

Rebecca sat back with her legs spread out. She unbuttoned the top two buttons of her shirt. Heslin took his off and ploughed through a couple of sandwiches as he finished his beer.

"Did you phone your agent?"

"He's still not speaking to me. I gave his secretary permission to use the s-word."

"Maybe you should have done that straight away."

"Maybe I wasn't sorry straight away."

"I like your arrogance."

"What arrogance?"

"Right there. Drink your beer, movie star," she said.

He scratched his chest tenderly, watching her on her back in the sun, smiling contentedly. Halfway through his second bottle, he asked her to tell him more about Browning.

"What do you want to know?"

"Everything."

"Alright," she said. "He plays bridge, drinks Scotch, killed my boyfriend, votes Tory, admires Ted Heath, never married and chases women impressed by his money and ambition. Only he doesn't have much money because he played too much bridge is what people are saying. When he took over this site, he cornered the market in paint manufacture. Now he has competition and his profits are dwindling."

"How do you know all this?"

"I read. I listen to people. If he can sell up, he'll make a lot of money and can pursue his political career."

"That's what I don't understand," Heslin said with his mouth full. "Has he said he's selling up?"

"Not in so many words."

"So these idiots down there could be striking over something that might not happen. How stupid can people be?"

"This coming from the man who's drinking at eleven in the morning over something that might not happen to him."

"Piss off. You said Keith worked there, didn't you? Hasn't he got any qualms about putting his colleagues on the breadline?"

"He needs the money like you and I. He said..."

"Let me guess, something about it being dog eat dog? The last refuge of a bastard."

Rebecca smiled at him.

"And how about you? How do you think Fred would feel about you profiting from his death?"

"Leave Fred out of this."

"Instead of this contrived little scheme, do you know what'd be a better way of getting over this Fred business and getting some money for it? Write to Dear Katie in the *TV Times*. You get a fiver for *Letter Of The Week*."

"I said leave him…"

"Why? He's the reason this started, isn't he? He's the reason we're sitting here now talking about destroying the livelihood of God knows how many families. Isn't he? We're here because your idiot boyfriend didn't follow the Green Cross Code one night when he was plastered."

Rebecca slowly took her shades off to get a look at him, her excessive eyeshadow giving her a real haunted look. "You're sitting here now," she said quietly. "Because in words of one syllable, Luke – you talk too much. Don't forget that."

They sat and stared at each other. Rebecca with her way of twisting things.

"You wish you'd never set eyes on me, don't you?" she said quietly.

He nodded. "If we mess this up," he murmured, "we're all going down for a very long time. Do you understand? No, don't interrupt, listen. What did you tell me about this Norman Browning? He can get out of drink-driving charges, yeah? He can escape manslaughter charges, right? The man's got so much influence, and this is what *you* told *me*, remember? The man's got so much influence there are policemen fitting perverts up to cover his crimes? He's protected from on high. When he got out of that car a few minutes ago and saw his workforce going out of their minds at his gates, you didn't see what he did."

"What?"

"He smiled. He actually smiled. You know what that tells me?"

"He's fearless."

"Exactly."

"He won't be fearless when he's eating porridge."

Heslin finished his bottle, needing another. "Look, Rebecca. I agree, yeah? Any man who grins at stuff like that down there deserves to have his arse felt in the prison showers. But if you want revenge, why don't you find some other way to get it? So other people don't lose out."

"I hear you, movie star but now *you* listen. The *only* way anything'll stick to Norman – I mean, Browning – is if everyone hates him. If he deprives the town of breadwinners, he's finished. It's the way things work. Now, I need money. It's that simple. I need it, Keith needs it and you need it. What do you care about them being unemployed? There's a recession on. They'll be out of work in a month or two anyway. Will you really care when we're on a beach in the south of France?"

"We?"

"You and I, movie star, you and I. Will you care when we're spending Christmas in Bordeaux and your birthday in Nice?"

"I've never even... You're confusing me. You want me to come abroad with you after this? Me?"

"Look, everything I've done over the last two days," she said smiling, that warmth finally returning, "is a first for me. I don't pick up just any men around the back of pubs or any of that *other* stuff. Now come to me."

Heslin took a deep breath and let out a huge sigh. Rebecca lay back, taking his face in her hands and pulling him down onto her, wrapping her legs round his.

He began to kiss her neck softly and she ran her fingers through his hair.

"Come on," she said. "Let's go back now."

"In a minute."

"What I said earlier," she murmured as he ran his hands gently up her side, "about how you felt yesterday? I didn't need to ask. I know how you felt."

"Go on," he said, moving onto her lips.

"Helpless," Rebecca said with a smile. "You felt totally helpless."

Christ, how he hated this bitch.

SEVEN

Wednesday Night

To be honest, I really wasn't in the mood for meeting the actor that night.

I still wasn't sold on him, still didn't want him coming in with us and when I saw *The Third Man* was on the telly, I just wanted to stay in. Cracking film that. Jim Mudd saw it when it first came out.

When I finished my free feed from Hing Lung's, I turned the telly off and walked across town to the Collier's Arms. There were a fair few in, including a lot from Browning's. Some of the butch women too.

I nodded at those who saw me, got my pint and went over to the fruit machine. Luke wasn't in yet but I was early so couldn't hold that against him.

"Got your records back yet, chief?" the barman – I couldn't remember his name – asked me.

"Have I fuck. The coppers probably aren't even looking for 'em."

"That's no good."

"Tell me about it. I can't work without 'em."

"You need a job?"

"Yeah. You got one going?"

"Afraid not, chief. Millions without, y'know."

"Is that supposed to cheer me up?"

"Just saying."

"Thing is, it's not just cos I don't get gigs but I miss having 'em on at my place. I have to keep the telly on just for some noise."

"You live by yourself?"

"It's me mate's gaff above the Picture Palace. Nice place, get a right view from the roof."

"Of what?" the barman said, pulling a pint for this bird. "Chimneys and smoke?"

"Birds."

"So where you looking for work then?"

"Me mate at Browning's is keeping his eye out and I'm meeting someone about a job tonight. He's late."

The doors swung open and Luke walked in like he owned the place, wearing a beige suit, wide flares and a shirt with a massive collar. He took his green shades off and looked over the place, checking it out and nodding at me. The barmaid went to serve him.

"Look at that clown," the barman said. "Thinks he's Robert Redford."

"That's who I'm meeting."

"Really? About a job? What's the job?" he said with a wink.

"Alright mate," I snapped. "I'm still a customer."

He grinned at me and said Luke looked familiar and that he'd told him to turn the radio down a few days ago. "From round here, is he?"

"He were. He went south."

"To do what?"

"Act, I think."

"That's it," he said. "I knew it. He were in that police thing on the telly last month. *Detroit Bobby* or something. Did you see it?"

"*Motown Cop*. Yeah."

The barman was shaking his head when Luke came over. "Can't believe they did that to a Jag."

"Keith," Luke said, holding out his hand.

We shook and I mumbled that I liked his suit.

"Shall we sit down?" he said.

"Here," the barman said, "can I just say? I right liked you on the telly. That were good: 'I shoot first and if I can think of a question, I'll ask it later'. Made the wife and me smile."

"Thanks," Luke said, nodding. "I came up with that line."

The barman folded his arms, grinning from ear to ear and just staring at Luke like he was Jesus himself or someone. Luke looked awkward and raised his eyebrows at me.

"See you later," I said to the barman and me and Luke moved to some stools by the fire. I didn't know how this was gonna go.

"What you drinking?"

"Outlaw," he said. "Locally brewed, isn't it? I haven't had it in years."

"I thought actors were gin drinkers."

"Just the queer ones," he said, smiling for about a second.

"Not you then, eh?"

Luke shook his head. "The woman in *Motown Cop*?"

And that was all he said, smiling and raising his pint.

"What, really? You and her."

67

"Me and her. Fay Barratt."

"Are you going out with her? She's tasty."

"I don't go out with anyone," he said. "It kind of limits your options, if you know what I mean?"

"Lucky bastard."

"She didn't put out at first. I thought I'd have to make an appointment but she soon came round to the idea."

Shaking my head, I said, "So what you doing up here then?"

"Rebecca didn't tell you? I'm hiding out until some shit blows over."

"She said something... Hey, you know when that S-type ended up in the river?"

"S-type? I don't..."

"In your show? Did they leave it in there or fish it out?"

"The Jaguar? Oh yeah, we pulled it out. They gutted the inside, sorted it all out and gave it to Estes as a birthday present. He got pulled over three times in one afternoon by policemen who couldn't believe a coloured hadn't nicked a motor like that."

"Christ, I never got given anything that big."

Luke rubbed his chest softly, grimacing. "From what she tells me, we're both gonna get something big when this is over."

I finished my dregs and put the pint pot down. "Fifteen hundred wage packets," I said quietly. "Five hundred each. In cash. That'll keep us going, eh?"

"We can't say much in here."

"I know. Most of this lot work at Browning's. Don't wanna get overheard, do we?"

"Yeah. Look, do you know your way around? In and out?"

"Like the back of me hand. I could get us into that office seen by no-one even if everyone were in that night and they were all looking for us. Pint?"

"Yeah, here."

He threw some coins down and I went to the bar, coughing on some bloke's smoke in my face next to me.

This Luke seemed alright, one of the lads. He stuck out like a sore thumb in that suit and, looking over at him, I thought he looked like he could strut sitting down but he didn't act up his own arse like you'd have thought.

"Look," I said, putting the pints down, "don't get pissed off or anything but this plan of hers... ours... I wouldn't have thought it were something an actor'd get involved in. It's more something for a... scrap merchant or someone. Not an actor."

"You saying I'm soft?"

"No. Just... how come you got involved?"

"Let's just say she talked me round," he said with a wink.

Bastard. He'd only been here a few days and shagged the bitch already. I wondered if he'd had to listen to her going on about Fred Dryden every time she'd had a drink too. Fair play though – the *Motown Cop* bird *and* Rebecca – the man did alright for himself.

"You staying at hers?"

He nodded.

"I take it you know everything then? Fred and all that?"

"Yeah. If some bastard knocked down my old lady, I'd wanna fill them in too."

"Me too."

"Have you got a bird?"

"I did have. Kelly."

He looked like he wanted me to say more.

"She went with someone behind me back."

"That's shit."

"Yeah."

"Did you sort him out for it?"

"In a way. What kind of crap are you in down south?"

"All sorts." Luke sighed. "To cut a long story short, I pissed off someone who has my balls in his hand. Only I didn't just piss him off as in privately, privately piss him off. I said things I shouldn't have."

"What kind of things?"

"He's a bad man. I expect to read all about him in the papers any day now. When I do, that's me finished for good. A bad, bad man."

He wanted to sound cocky when he said it, I could tell. Wanted to sound like he was fine with it but his face gave him away. He looked nervous as fuck and took a big drink to hide it. He was scared.

"Tell him to fuck off."

"It's rarely that easy. You ever heard of John Gilbert?"

"Works at the sheet metal foundry, course I have."

"Not him. This one was a… Sod it. Never mind."

"No, tell me."

He took a long drink and gently touched his chest. "There was this actor in the twenties, John Gilbert. A silent actor. Massive. As big as a star could be back then and every woman everywhere wanted to bed him. On his wedding day, you heard of Greta Garbo?"

"Yeah, she were a right piece."

"He was marrying her. Except she didn't turn up. The head of his studio, a man called Louis Mayer, told

Gilbert in the loo, don't marry her but keep screwing her. So Gilbert floors him. One punch. Down. Mayer gets up and he's proper pissed off and tells Gilbert he's gonna have him for it."

"Why didn't he just lay one on him back?"

"He might have done, I don't know. This story got told to me by some playwright one night. I might have parts wrong. Anyway, they start making sound films soon and when Gilbert appears in one, suddenly the women don't wanna screw him anymore. Because his voice doesn't fit his looks. Handsome bloke, squeaky voice. He becomes this laughing stock. And he stops getting film work. And people start talking about him when his back's turned. And he turns to drink. And he gets depressed, grows a beard. His career goes arse up."

"Cos he had a bird's voice?"

"Because he punched the wrong man."

"Yeah, but... Go on."

"His voice," Luke said, taking a swig. "There's nothing wrong with it. Yeah, it's not brilliant but it's not shit like people were led to believe. This geezer told me Mayer got so pissed off at Gilbert, he went the extra mile to shaft his career. Is that Sparks?"

He held up his hand, listening out to the radio.

"Oi mate, turn that shit off!" someone shouted.

The radio went dead and Luke carried on. "Rumours started that Mayer starts creeping into the sound booth, paying the technicians to screw with Gilbert's voice so it sounds worse on film. That sets the ball rolling and soon the bloke can't get any work. All because he punched someone with a lot of influence."

"So?"

"I'm in a similar situation to John Gilbert. He punched his gaffer. I did something potentially much more damaging to mine. You wanna know how much shit I'm in?"

"Yeah."

"If I'm lucky, he'll only wreck my career. If I'm really lucky, he'll let me live."

"Really?"

Luke nodded, mumbling that maybe he'd said too much.

"Powerful bloke, your gaffer then, eh? Like Browning."

Luke smiled.

"So, this other actor? This John Gilbert? He didn't appear in any more films then?"

"One or two." Luke went, finishing his drink. "They were shit. Pint?"

Luke told a good story, I'll give him that. It was weird sitting across from someone you'd seen on the telly though. Even weirder than when you met footballers in the Visage. To me anyway. Rebecca probably wasn't impressed by him – she'd met The Faces.

"Here's a question for you," he said when he sat down again. "What's going on with this pub?"

"How do you mean?"

"The barman offered me coffee and a roll this morning. Is that a new northern thing?"

"Not northern mate, no. He went to France for the first time a couple of month back and come home with a load of foreign ideas. Fucking coffee and a roll."

"Guaranteed way to lose customers."

"Yeah."

We drank a fair bit, not speaking. He went off to the loo and I sat watching everyone again, thinking of more stuff to ask him.

"Anything else you can tell me?" I said when he got back.

"Like what?"

"Other secrets?"

"Connery co-owns a car dealership in the East End and Hughie Green's not Canadian. Oh, and Britt Ekland..."

He was about to tell me another story when I felt arms around my neck and stubble touch my face.

"What the... Jim?"

"You try again!"

"Aldo," I said, removing his arms, relieved he wasn't Jim Mudd come to ruin my night. "Aldo the Eyetie."

He was pissed, bless him, wearing his only suit, shirt open to show off his rug and medallions. "I am celebrating," he said, clutching his bottle of whatever. "You know why?"

"Cos you've got me a job?"

"Because I am going to be a father!"

"Fuckin' Hell, Aldo, that's great news. That's really... great news. Congratulations," I said, shaking his hand and feeling – for a moment anyway – a bit jealous.

"I thank you, Keef," he said and pulled my cheek. "Who is your friend? I like his suit."

"Luke, Aldo."

Luke stood and they shook hands.

"Aldo's one of the foremen at Browning's, y'know the paint factory on the outskirts?"

"Yeah, I think so," he said, proper actor's voice. "Used to be Lyons?"

"I wouldn't know," Aldo said. "I have only been here for one year. Now I am going to drink with my friends until I fall over. Nice to meet you, Luke."

"You too."

The daft sod stumbled off into the smoke behind me.

"One of the nicest blokes you could hope to meet," I said. "We got matey living round Coggy's during the Three Day Week. He gave me the plans."

"Him? Jesus, doesn't he suspect...?"

"Not Aldo. Typical Italian, believes and does what he's told. Need to go and splash me boots."

I wandered into the loo, seeing Peter Jenkins carving *Browning Is Scum* into the wall with his knife. "He's gonna sell us down the river, I'm telling you," Jenko said as he walked out. "He's all arse and no soul."

Jenko used to sit behind me in maths and carve his name into everything. He was amazing at drawing, could have gone to Art College. Instead he had a kid at fourteen and now worked twelve hours loading lorries.

I thought, sorry Jenko but everyone was gonna suffer when we hit that place, you included. The fallout was gonna be huge but I'd said it before and I'll say it again: it's a dog eat dog world.

All in all I was having a good night. Not too pissed but relaxed and ready to get on and get rich.

Then I opened the door and saw Kidney at the bar with three mates. He was looking all over the pub, fury in his black eyes and plasters on his head.

Christ, what was he doing out? He'd swung at a copper last night. Were the cells full or something?

The door closed and I looked round to the windows. They were too narrow to get through. I was trapped. I couldn't even poke my head round to see if he went outside or round the back. There were four of them – one would definitely spot me.

I went into one of the cubicles and locked the door behind me, sitting just as the door to the gents opened.

Crouching down, I saw four pairs of feet come in and my heart went through my mouth and up into the sky. My breathing got faster and I had to cover my mouth.

"Sod it, Stake Junior," one said. "He's not here, is he?"

"It's his boozer, he'll be in later. We'll have a few pints and wait for the little bastard to turn up."

"The look on his face, eh? 'Alright boys, how come you're out?'"

They all laughed.

I knew why they were out. It was the same reason they didn't get charged or brought to court. Because the coppers agreed with them. If this lot got a desk sergeant who also hated the foreigners, they'd have got breakfast in bed this morning.

"Let's...," Kidney or Stake or whatever his name was began, "Oi oi."

"You alright in there mate?" one said. "Been on the ale, have you?"

One booted my cubicle door and I wanted to be sick. The lock only just held. "Oi mate, he asked you a question."

I kept schtum.

They were whispering.

"It's not gonna be him."

"It is. Have a look."

There was a pause then, "Oi, you in there. Do you always crock a solid with your trousers up?"

Oh Christ, Luke, get in here now and floor these bastards *Motown Cop*-style. One or two and I'm fine but four and I'm a dead man and that free Chinky was *not* worth getting my head caved in.

Kidney piped up, telling me I had five seconds to open the door before he broke it down, adding he didn't wanna chin me, he was just looking for someone.

Yeah, I know, I thought, you just found him.

I took a deep breath.

"I'm coming," I said slowly in a voice that sounded nothing like me.

Two beatings in one week, Christ.

I slid the lock back and let the door swing open, still sitting on the bog as all four eyeballed me. "If it isn't fuckin' Pete's Pocket Army," I said.

"Here he is," Kidney snarled, and came into the cubicle, grabbing my lapels and wrenching me out. He threw me clear across the floor and I smacked into the urinal.

"I'm gonna enjoy this. Think yesterday were clever, do you? Getting Chang and his family to shut up shop? You fuckin' will do!" He backhanded me across the face and reached into his belt for a screwdriver. "You long-haired bastard. Gimme a hand boys, we'll start by flushing the prick down there."

Two others moved in and grabbed my arms just as the door swung open and some old bloke stepped in.

He stopped still. "Here…"

"Get out," Kidney snapped.

The bloke looked at me, dopey as owt.

"Man in a sharp suit," I said, staring at him. "OK? Sharp. Beige. Suit?"

The bloke backed out and I hoped to God he'd got the message. It took Kidney a while to understand. He swung a punch at my head and the other two let me sag to the piss-wet floor. Kidney booted me in the ribs three times before the door swung open and Luke stepped in.

"Look lads," he said as they turned to look at him. "Are you out for trouble or are you out for a good time?"

"A good time," the one closest to him sniggered.

"Unlucky," Luke said and booted him in the balls.

I suppose – looking back – it was kinda funny how one of these skinheads recognised him from the telly just as Luke floored him like John Gilbert.

My ribs were caning too much for me to laugh though but from the floor, I saw Luke's elbow go into one of them's eye before he grabbed him and proper brought his face down on the sink – original street fighting man, this actor. The skinhead went down next to me and as the third one went for Luke, I swung my leg round, swept Kidney off his feet and then propelled – if you wanna use that word – both feet into his chest. He went backwards, I got up and booted the cubicle door into his face when he got up again.

It got kinda blurry after that but I do remember raining down blows on his face as his mate tried strangling me from behind. I got my elbow into his chest then chin and he tripped over the one out cold on the floor and landed in the urinal the moment it started to flush.

Luke headbutted his one and backed away, grabbing the wire bin in the corner and using it to smash the skinhead round the face – Wednesday night being more than alright for fighting.

As I shoved Kidney's head in the crapper, drowning him, I heard millions of angry footsteps ploughing into the pub. Suddenly the bogs were full of uniformed coppers, tonnes of them, smacking all five of us with truncheons.

The skinhead by the urinal dropped the knife he'd been about to slice me with. A copper bent his arm behind his back and I heard it snap. I saw Luke and the other go down as the coppers circled them then I was hit round the head and bent over a sink to be handcuffed.

"It's this prick again," one said as they hauled the bloody, groggy and damp Kidney out of the bog. "Knew he shouldn't have been let out."

All I'll say about the end of that night was my arresting officer was the copper on the desk from Monday. As he shoved me up against the wall outside, he asked if I'd got my records back yet.

EIGHT

Off The Books

The next morning, three policemen came into his cell and told him how much they admired *Motown Cop*.

One gave him tips on how to make it more realistic but overall, yeah, they were fans and hoped it got a series. After he signed autographs he sensed would soon be worthless, Heslin was released with Keith.

"I never got chance to say it last night," Keith said on the steps in the early morning sun, "but cheers for everything. You were brilliant. A proper mate."

"Forget about it," Heslin said, having warmed to this kid obsessed with his music. "Anyone would have done the same."

"No they wouldn't, that's the thing. Them bastards had screwdrivers and would have carved me up good and proper if you hadn't stepped in. Thanks mate. Listen, do you wanna come over later? I'll get us some cans."

"Cheers but I'm gonna have a wander back to Rebecca's, let her know we're alright. We're coming over one night anyway, aren't we?"

"Yeah," Keith said. "Alright, well cheers again. See you."

Heslin watched him walk up the street and cross, disappearing round a corner. He had balls, Keith Moran, a massive pair of balls.

Taking his change from his pocket and rubbing his tender chest, Heslin crossed over to a telephone box with glass panels missing and dialled Melanie. He heard her answer and struggled to get the coin in the slot. "Hi Mel, guess who? Is Dean around?"

Jesus, she sounded more nervous than usual – really uneasy, the bright and breezy tone gone. "He's out…"

"Is he though? Is he actually out or is he still fobbing me off? Because if he's there, Mel, put him on the bloody telephone, I'm sick of this pissing about. If he's there, put me through and don't lie to me."

"He isn't," she said. "Honestly. But Sidney wants you to call him."

"Sidney? Really?"

Sidney himself, thank God, *thank God*, he wants to speak personally.

Grovel Lucas, he told himself, as Melanie gave him the number, kiss his arse like you've never kissed arse before. He thanked Melanie, apologised for swearing then dialled, heart in his mouth or whatever the phrase was.

"Sidney King Productions, Samantha speaking, how can I help?"

"Luke Heslin for Mr. King, please Samantha," he said, sounding bold when he said his own name, daring her to ask what it was about.

"Two seconds, sugar," she said.

Heslin watched a couple of birds, about seventeen, walk past. He thought, for the rest of my life I'll be surrounded by your type, oh yes. Back on the telly, his own show, watching himself on Saturday nights. Sod this robbery, sod Rebecca. She'd understand. He could talk her round, telling her she'd be much richer sticking with him than by screwing Browning. If she wanted revenge on Browning, he could speak to the writers, get them to create a bastard and call him Norman Browning. Nasty but sweet. What woman wouldn't want him?

"Lucas, hi. Sidney. Thanks for calling."

"Mr. King," he said, knowing he'd sound too fast, "before you say anything, I wanna say I couldn't be more sorry for what I did, I was a bloody idiot. A fool. I didn't mean any of it, yeah? I pride myself on our relationship, you've always been important to me and I'm so sorry – and so sorry for swearing – but this matters to me more than you could imagine. There isn't a thing in the world I wouldn't do to put this right and I..."

"Lucas, just listen, alright? Listen."

"Yes sir."

"I've gagged them. It goes no further. I'm safe."

"Oh thank God, sir, I..."

"You let me down, Lucas..."

"I know I did and I'm more sorry than you could..."

"Lucas..."

"Sorry."

"Lucas, let's talk shop. *Motown Cop*'s moving into production next month. Sixteen episodes. I'm gonna be a busy man indeed. It's shooting throughout autumn, going out in January."

Heslin felt gratitude sweep all over him. He wanted to cry tears of relief or something. Oh Jesus, it was more than worth getting sunburned and punched to hear this. He could escape this northern craphouse and never ever come back. Nice meeting you, Keith, hope you get your records back. Sod it, he was gonna quit the booze too. He was gonna get fit and healthy, become the sexiest policeman on the telly.

"The sky's the limit on this, Lucas. We're spending forty-five grand an episode, we're going gritty, we're getting retired Scotland Yarders in as consultants and I'm negotiating with a writer from Detroit to punch up Estes' dialogue."

"Make the Yank sound more Yank?"

"Exactly. I hired Toby Thompson and Dan Meleady as script editors this morning."

"Great writers, I heard."

"Like I said, the sky's the limit, Lucas. This is all good but you're really not gonna believe the best thing about it."

"What?"

"Guess."

"I... erm, don't know. What?"

"*You*, sunshine, are not in it."

"You what? What...?"

"We cast Mickey Fleming yesterday."

"My part...?"

"We open with your funeral. Final enough for you?"

"But... I wrote..."

Sidney laughed. "I get a coloured in my cast and it's the honky who blabs. You're finished, Lucas. Your name has so much manure attached to it, you can stick it on your rhubarb. You couldn't even get a job narrating British Transport films. Get used to being the feral dog of my industry now, sunshine. Come within a mile of my studio and I'll have you buried beneath several tonnes of gravel out at Maplin Sands."

"Listen Sid..."

"No Lucas, *you* listen. Thursday was merely a goddamn *aperitif* of what I could have done to you. You're lucky I'm not having your kneecaps ripped off. Believe me, I needed a *lot* of talking out of that. By Christmas, you'll be begging for parts in pantomime in... whichever northern dump you came from. Is this coming through clear enough? I could have made you a supernova, Lucas, massive on both sides of the pond but you took the lifeline I threw you and..."

"Sidney, Mr. King, please? You don't know how sorry I am for all this, please just gimme a chance, just one tiny chance..."

His voice was cracking, all vulnerability and fear.

"You had your chance, Lucas. Your treachery is costing you. The beauty of it is I know how hard you worked to get here and I know just how badly this'll haunt you for the rest of your pathetic, alky life. The only good thing is it'll cement your friendship with Lazenby. Go speak to him, he knows all about biting the hand that feeds him. You'll have some laughs together. Wave bye to the fanny too. After all this, you couldn't even poke Britt Ekland down a telephone line let alone the proper way. Oh, and don't forget to watch the programme every Saturday night from whichever gutter you wind up in, will you?" Sid said and laughed. "Now piss off."

The line went dead.

Oh shit...

Heslin felt that absolute, total panic washing over him, that utter dread and regret that stung a million times more than any sunburn. His lip started quivering as he gently cradled the receiver.

Blackness.

His whole... everything was going black, *was* black. Oh Jesus, a whole life to live knowing he'd screwed up everything and couldn't get it back.

Oh shit...

He sank to the floor of the telephone box, sticking his head between his knees and staying like that. Trying his hardest not to cry, trying his hardest to think of someone else he could blame, trying his hardest to think of someone else who had it worse than him right now.

Luke Heslin on the cutting room floor of his own world – an exile from the only career he'd wanted – the only thing that had ever mattered to him.

Oh shit...

What felt like years later, with cramp in his legs, he stood up and dialled Melanie. "Yes or no, Mel. Did you know about it?"

"What?"

"Yes? Or no?"

She paused. "Honestly Luke, Dean begged him and begged him."

"Did you know?"

"He tried..."

"And you couldn't have told me before I phoned Sid? Before you threw me to him? Cheers Mel, some friend. You know what you are? You're a bitch. They laugh at you when your back's turned..."

"Luke..."

"'Look at Mel, like a timid field mouse, never made a decision in her life, turned up to the Christmas party in her granny's dress, still got her V-plates on, can't get a man...' That's only a tenth of what they say."

He really needed to hurt someone.

When she started to cry, Dean came on the line, telling her to take five minutes. "She didn't deserve that, Luke. She's worked her arse off for you so don't you ever speak to her like that again. Not that you'll get chance."

"Let me guess," he spat. "Suddenly I'm no longer with you."

"In your parlance, Luke: you blew it. Train as a plumber. It's over."

Heslin slammed the telephone down, dug out more change and dialled Fay.

No reply.

Frantic now, he dug out his remaining coins and hedged his bets: Jack the writer or Estes the star? Jack or Estes, who had more influence? "Not the writer," he murmured, dialling one more number. "Never the writer."

"Yo."

"Estes, it's Luke."

"Oh…"

"Don't *oh* me. You've heard what they did?"

Silence.

"Estes?"

"I heard, brother, yeah. Man, it a real shame, really enjoy working wit' you."

"I need you to ring Sid, right? I need you to ring him and tell him you won't go back unless I'm in it. I'll call you back in five minutes."

"I can't do that, Lucas. I can't…"

"What do you mean? Can't or won't?"

"Look man, they even hear I been speaking to you, I get fined and they stick some of the shit they sticking on you on me, yeah? I can't afford no shit on my back, brother, I'm sorry."

"Please…"

"Lucas," Estes said, sighing. "They burnt your digs this morning, man."

Heslin froze. "They what?"

"Your flat, man. They torch that mother, it… I don't know *exactly* who did it but I can guess."

"My things…," Heslin said, his voice quivering. "What about all my belongings?"

"Don't know, man. You a nice guy, Lucas. I like you but I ain't risking my neck for nobody, no sir. You understand?"

"No I don't bloody understand! You have to say a few words, that's all. We're a team. We're a package. Tell Sid that."

"Look man, I gotta go."

"You ungrateful… You bloody ungrateful nigger! I should have let those Nazis in Soho put your eyes out."

"What you call me? I say, the fuck you…?"

Heslin smashed the receiver down.

After he vandalised the telephone box, ripped down the sign telling him to dial carefully and wrenched the receiver out, Heslin headed to the park, praying to whoever for a way out of this mess.

His head spinning, he wound up on the swing he'd spent hours on as a child, staring at the deserted roundabout and empty slide with that sun on the back of his sweaty neck.

Somewhere in the distance, a church bell tolled ten o'clock and he put his head in his hands, promising himself that in one hour he'd be in a pub drinking himself to death.

Eventually, he became aware of voices nearby and a child laughing. He turned to see a couple and a little girl coming over to the roundabout. He recognised them too and his heart sank.

Fiona Wilks and Albert Pearce. God, he hadn't seen them in years. In fact the last time he had seen her, was naked and even that didn't make him smile. He wondered if she was still frigid until she drank. He wondered too why she'd settled for Albert Pearce. She hated him at school. If the kid grew up looking like daddy, she was screwed. Ugly bastard. Albert, you... Stop it, Luke, he thought, it isn't their fault you...

"Luke Heslin, what on earth?"

He waved as Fiona walked towards him, smiling with her yellow halter-neck dress and curly blonde hair. "Luke Heslin in a suit. Aren't we a big shot?"

Albert was pushing the kid on the roundabout, staring over at them. Heslin thought about punching him for old times' sake and to make himself feel better. Bloody Hell, where were those Nazis when he needed to let off steam?

"You look like you slept in it."

"I did," he said, staring up at her in her NHS frames. "How's it going, Fiona?"

She sat on the swing beside his. "It's going very well, thank you. I'm a receptionist at Addie's Dentist. Not bad money, renting a nice house, been seeing Albert for a few years, got a lovely nine year-old, that's her there, and it's all going very well," she said without pausing. It all sounded so rehearsed and unconvincing, she might as well have stuck *honest* on the end. She hadn't changed at all – still never asked about you.

"That's great. Addie's Dentist," he muttered.

"What's wrong with that?"

"Nothing Fiona, I was just saying…"

"Just cos I'm not on the bleeding telly, alright? Just cos I'm not this big star? So what if I am only a receptionist, at least I've got a job. Loads haven't. Albert's a driver for Cartledge's, good money and you don't…"

"Fiona, in the nicest possible way, shut up. I was just saying the name of your employer, alright? Jesus, bloody northerners are so sensitive these days. We used to be tough not… shirty."

"You were being…"

"I wasn't being anything. Now shut up and give me a Fiona Wilks smile."

Career or not, he still had it. She grinned broadly and it took him right back.

"It's nice to see you again, Luke," she said. "You're looking… There's red on your jacket."

"I had to chin someone. Albert Pearce, eh?"

"He's grown up a *lot*."

"That must be a big relief."

"Although when we saw you on the telly last month, Albert went, 'No way could Luke pull that bird in real life'," she said, grinning.

"Albert said that, did he?" Heslin said, watching him push the kid on the roundabout and making stupid noises with it. "You should tell Albert he couldn't be more wrong." And he looked right in her eyes and held her gaze.

"You *never*…"

"Maybe tell Albert that the next time I hear any more shit like that from him, you and I'll pick up where we left off."

Fiona went red. "Luke…"

Her mouth opened slightly and there was a brief moment when he was eighteen again – when they were both eighteen, and he was confident not cocky, certain of himself but not needing to mouth off to prove it.

"You shouldn't say things like that," Fiona said with that smile. "He might hear you."

They watched Albert, still at the roundabout, Heslin wondering why he wasn't at work. Fiona said that *Motown Cop* had been right good, hadn't it?

"I wasn't impressed myself."

"You were never modest, what's happened? Hey, they mentioned you in her school assembly the day after it were on. Mrs. Ohlsen still teaches there. Do you remember that time she sent you out in the rain for talking?"

"Fancy me getting in trouble for having a big mouth."

"So, what you been up to since you left me sleeping?"

"In your mother's bed."

"In me mam's bed. With a hangover. You still owe her for the drainpipe by the way."

He'd forgotten about that – the eighteen-year-old Luke still drunk, assuming it could take his weight.

"And you never called me. You swine, you said you would. Instead of just sodding off down south."

"Why don't we go somewhere now and I'll make it up to you?" he said.

"Luke!"

He almost smiled. He couldn't be arsed to apologise any more today. So what if she was still upset over something that happened all those years ago?

"Well, this has been delightful," he said, standing up. "Take care. Oh and in case you still see any of the girls from school, I'm seeing…"

"Who?" she said, eyes wide.

Heslin looked at her – Fiona trapped here forever – and shook his head.

"Never you mind." He nodded towards Albert, taking the kid off the roundabout. "What's your little girl called?"

"Emily. Emily Amber Wilks. Emily after me mam and Amber after her dad's mam."

"Nice. Take care, yeah?"

"You too."

Albert insisted on shaking his hand when he walked past, calling him mate, Heslin thinking, grown up or not, you're still a snot-nosed bastard. He managed a hello to the kid but that was all.

At the gate, he turned to see all three of them at the swings. Albert pushing the kid and Fiona staring right at him. She raised her hand and waved briefly.

He nodded, turned, and left them to it.

He was surprised he wasn't barred from the Collier's Arms and even more surprised when his pint was on the house as the barman hated skinheads.

"They wanna act like animals, chief, they can do it up *le* Plough. Although you owe me for a new sink," he said.

"How about I train as a plumber and fix it for free?"

"Eh?"

"Never mind."

"I'll get it sorted and we'll discuss payment next time you're in."

Seven minutes past eleven and he was the only customer. The Osmonds on the radio.

The barman said, "Thinking about getting a pool table in here. It'd mean less space for the drinkers but

I reckon that'd be a nice feature. What do you think, chief?"

"I could have done with a pool cue last night."

"I hear you were quite handy with your fists. Really know how to mix it, don't you? You wouldn't think it to look at you."

"Somewhere I worked, you got stabbed in the back all the time if you weren't careful."

"Not many men wear suits to fight in. Laddo were telling me you and him are gonna be working together."

"Yeah. Just the one job for a bit of cash."

"Squiring the older ladies? They pay more, they get more."

"You asking if I screw for money?"

"Alright chief, just joking with you."

"I know," Heslin said and forced a grin. "Me too. What bus do I get to…?"

"Hang on," the barman said, turning the radio up. "What's this?"

"Breaking news now," someone was saying, "and in a surprise move announced only this morning, Norman Browning has stated that he will not be selling up his paint factory to clear alleged gambling debts. Workers and unions were worried this would lead to a loss of around fifteen hundred jobs. Rumours have been rife for weeks now that the factory would be bulldozed to make way for a housing estate."

"Bloody Hell," the barman muttered. "Never saw that coming."

Browning Browning Browning and his bloody paint factory. Norman Browning and Sidney King – the only two names Heslin seemed to hear these days. Both a pair of bastards.

What must have been Browning came on with, "It were never my intention to sell the factory nor were it my intention to make my private business public. I believe that the lies and misinformation spread among my workforce were a calculated plot by the TGWU designed to undermine my authority and bring production of paint in the north of this country to a complete halt. However, I will be putting this business behind me now and look forward to forging ahead with my employees to create a brighter future."

Sounding every inch an ambitious Tory, Heslin thought. What a prick.

"Quite the day for job news," he said, finishing his pint.

"You what, chief? Oh yes. That'll be a massive relief. There'll be some celebrating going on in here tonight. They say Browning's the kind of bloke who has gravy on his fish."

Heslin nodded – relieved this man didn't want to talk to him about the bloody cop programme.

"Good job too," the barman said. "Some of the regulars reckoned they were gonna stick him in a giant wicker man and burn it down. You seen that film?"

"Seen it?" Heslin said, opening the door. "I was in it."

Then he went out into the sunshine, heading for the bus depot and remembering that Amber had been his mother's name.

NINE

Being Needed

Rebecca assumed they'd spent the night watching *Sportsnight* at Keith's and smiled when he told her about the policemen wanting his autograph.

He got the Smirnoff out and went into the sun lounge with her following him. She removed her silky robe and hung it on a hook by the door, sitting in a wicker chair in her underwear, crossing her legs. Her black eye was still coated in eyeshadow.

He said, "Is it weird to find arms attractive?"

She shook her head. "Tell me your story," she said.

He told her everything. She listened patiently and didn't interrupt, letting him get it all out right up to arriving back here.

"I need money," Heslin said at the end.

"You'll have it soon. Your suit needs cleaning. Why don't you take it off?"

He took off his jacket, draped it over the back of a chair and unbuttoned his shirt, revealing his red raw chest.

"It still looks painful. Is it?"

"Stings like crazy. It chafes."

"I could run you a cold bath."

"I'd be tempted to drown myself," he said, looking out at the smashed camp bed leant against the garage.

"Why don't you have a nice soak in the tub and I'll go out for wine. We can spend the afternoon in the sun. Just the two of us."

"You'd have to put clothes on if you went out," he said, hoping that sounded cool.

She said, "Not necessarily," and went into the house.

Heslin smiled. The panic had subsided a bit now. Maybe Sidney would calm down completely. Maybe that prick Mickey Fleming would screw up the role – the rushes showing he wasn't photogenic or something. Maybe this was the vodka speaking, telling him his messed up world wasn't so messed up after all. Maybe a cold bath would calm him down.

Rebecca reappeared all in denim, her hair tied back. "I want you stripped, bathed and scented for me when I return," she said.

"If I admit this is a stupid question, can I ask it?"

She nodded.

"Is there any way out of this huge mess?"

"There's a way out of everything. Yours involves Mr. Browning. Now take your clothes off and let me get a good look at you."

From an upstairs window, he watched the Scimitar burn off and as the bath was running, he wandered round the house, room to room. The spare bedrooms were empty, all floorboards, built-in wardrobes and woodchip wallpaper. Candles all over the place, a couple of butane lamps too, just waiting for the next power cut.

There was only her bedroom that seemed to have much in it: dressing table, double bed, two wardrobes covering a whole wall. There was a Faces gig poster on the back of the door along with tickets for The Who and Elton. Beneath those was a yellow flyer for Westerton's Soul Nite – Keith Moran DJ'ing.

Heslin opened the wardrobe, not expecting to find anything, hoping perhaps for a photo of her from college or maybe a photo of Fred Dryden. But hoping more to find her photos of the movie star.

Nothing.

He sniffed a few of her dresses, his eyes closed and thought when this was all over and they were on the Riviera he might be happy again. She was stunning and clever enough – not a bimbo, all breasts and no conversation. She might have told him she had a degree too – biology, was it?

After a quick look at her shoe rack, he brought up the vodka and some matches, getting the *Motown Cop* script from his suitcase. He took it into the bathroom and sat on the loo, staring at the front page:

> *Evidence Of A Dying Love*
> [*Motown Cop*, episode #2]
>
>
> by
>
>
> Jack Henshaw
> &
> Lucas Heslin

03/07/74

Heslin poured a large vodka and downed it in one as he read the first page yet again. He didn't get further than

Estes making two arrests and dropping a pimp in a Soho brothel.

Dropping the script in the sink, he lit two corners and stood watching the flames eat away at the paper. He flicked a couple of spots of her Scherezade on to make it die faster. The last thing to be consumed was his name. At that point, he turned the taps on and climbed into the bath, his cock shrinking, the water was so cold.

He was wondering what would happen to all his fan mail, wondering what the bastards had hoped to achieve by torching his flat and wondering who was least happy – him or Fiona – when he heard the Scimitar pull up.

He climbed out, gently touching his tender burns, and rubbing himself dry. In her room, he dug out a pair of pants and took her green robe from the wardrobe, winking sadly at himself in the mirror.

Rebecca was putting two bottles of red on the rack and three white and a small bottle of Smirnoff in the fridge.

"Suits you," she said, nodding at her robe.

"Have you heard about Browning?"

"He's not selling up?" she said with that smile. "I heard it in the car earlier."

He followed her into the sun lounge, lying down with his head in her lap. She ran her fingers through his hair as she spoke. "This is perfect," she said. "This is better than we could have imagined. The fool has played right into my hands. Everyone loves him now – the place burns down and he can't prove he wasn't behind it – everyone hates him."

"He's shafted himself."

"More so than the man from *Motown Cop*," she said, leaning down and kissing him.

He lay there in silence for several minutes, eyes closed, totally relaxed with her.

"Have you ever been to Bordeaux?" she asked.

"Never."

"It's beautiful. You'll love it. Pretty architecture, so much to see and do, a café on every street corner. The nightlife puts ours to shame. Soon we'll be there. Walking down Rue St. Catherine hand in hand, I'm carrying a baguette and cooked meats for lunch. You have a bottle of wine. We can spend days in each other's arms, Luke. We don't even have to get out of bed if we don't want to."

"What's the point of going somewhere different if we're just gonna stay in bed?"

"Silly boy. Not every day, of course. People'll look at us and say 'Isn't that the man who was on the television all those years ago?'"

"I wanna be on the telly now."

"I know," she said, kissing his forehead. "We'll be the mysterious English couple whose neighbours gossip about them, wanting to know how we got our money."

"And you'd be happy doing all that continental cooking?"

She ignored him. "You can tell them you retired from acting because it didn't stretch you. I can be an heiress."

"Please tell me this Browning business can't be traced to us," he said, eyes still closed. "I don't want the gendarmes knocking on the door at three in the morning with a pair of warrants."

"Do you have to ruin it? I was painting such a nice picture."

"I can't speak French."

She patted his cheek. "I can, don't worry."

"I wonder what Keith'll do."

"Who knows? Rich at twenty-two. Can't be bad. He can buy his records again. Maybe run his own shop."

"Nice lad," Heslin said. "Quite the hard bastard too."

"That'll come in handy on Saturday."

"Saturday?"

"When you rob Browning."

Heslin sat up and stared at her.

She was almost smiling at him. "If your movie star friends could see you now. Wearing my robe…"

"What the Hell are you on about, Saturday? That's two days away. We need time to plan."

"Time to get cold feet, you mean."

"I've already got cold feet. Are you joking?"

Rebecca took a clump of his hair in her hand and pulled his head down to her lap, stroking him as he lay there, panicking but trying to relax under her caress. "There's no night shift on Saturday. There are only two watchmen who sit at the gate and take it in turns to patrol with torches every hour or so."

"Why this Saturday?" he murmured.

"Because we're all running out of money. We'll meet Keith tomorrow, he can show you the plans and then you're all set."

"Bloody Hell."

"He has a balaclava helmet for himself. You can have a pair of tights for your head."

"Sod that, I want a balaclava. Those villains in *Motown Cop* wore tights when they pulled that blag at the start and they still got recognised. Tights do nothing for you. I'm having his balaclava."

"They'll recognise him," Rebecca said, tracing a line around his mouth with her finger. "He used to work there."

"They'll recognise me."

"You're not as famous as you think you are."

"Eleven million viewers, Rebecca. Second billing and tonnes of close-ups. That's pretty bloody famous."

"Well, if you can get a balaclava…"

"Where would I get a balaclava from in August?"

"Give Tricky Dicky a ring, he might have a few left over."

Heslin sighed. Reaching up, he unbuttoned her denim shirt and kissed her bare breasts, shifting to get more comfortable. As he buried his head, she slipped the robe from his shoulders. He murmured that she was beautiful and she asked him to say it again properly.

"I said I hate you for getting me involved in this," he said with a smile.

Their eyes met and she looked vulnerable for the first time since he'd known her. Gazing up at him, waiting for him to say more. He leant in for a kiss.

"If you hadn't ruined your career, we'd never have met."

"I know."

"Was I worth it?"

He nodded.

She cupped his face between her hands and pushed him to the side, him sitting back as she straddled him, working to get her jeans open, kissing him nonstop and not giving him time to breathe. Rebecca stood up to strip and seconds later, she was on the floor, naked beneath him.

Briefly, Heslin wondered whether he should send Fiona a few notes for the upkeep of the kid.

Afterwards, they lay on their backs breathing heavily, covering their eyes from the sun pouring through the roof.

"Where did you meet Fred?"

"Hmmn?"

"Fred? Where did you meet him?"

"At a garden fete. Let's not talk about him," she said. "He's gone."

"Why won't you…?"

"Luke…"

"Did you love him?"

Rebecca slowly got up and sat in the wicker chair, gazing out at the garden. "Does it matter?" she said quietly. "Would you be jealous if I did?"

A few days earlier and he'd have wounded her with a remark about never being jealous of someone who'd got run over. But he was thinking differently now. More clearly? Maybe.

"Not jealous but…"

She still wasn't looking at him, still sitting and watching the grass grow. Mouthy Luke Heslin was finally lost for words.

"Go on," she said.

"Not jealous," he said. "But… for you to do all this for him, he must have really had a hold on you."

'Had a hold on you'? he thought. Oh shit, Luke, she's making you quote songs now

"Something like that."

From where he lay he could see her just staring out, her bare arms folded, bare legs crossed, bare foot making a slow circular motion.

"You're putting everything at risk to avenge him yet you can't even bring yourself to speak to me about him."

She looked down at him, eyes narrowed and cold. "Take the hint, movie star."

Heslin sighed.

They sat in silence for five minutes. Awkward silence.

"When I saw you in the Colliery Arms," Heslin said, needing to speak before he fell asleep, "when you were eyeing me up..."

"*You* were eyeing me up."

"No I wasn't."

"You were."

"Why would I be eyeing you up, I was the one on the telly. That's the way it were."

"*Were?*" she laughed. "Tut tut, your accent's slipping."

"*Was* then. That's the way it was."

"Your arrogance, movie star. You and your arrogance."

He grinned at her. A smile slowly came to her lips. She unfolded her arms and put her hands on the arms of the chair. Her foot stopped circling.

"I have to admit," Rebecca said. "You can be one smooth bastard."

"Thanks."

"Are you in love with me yet?"

Heslin laughed. "A little bit. Perhaps. You?"

"'A little bit' really won't do."

"I think I'd probably do almost anything for you after this afternoon. Does that help?"

"Is this your roundabout way of telling me I can make you happy?"

"Under the circumstances."

"I think you've got sunstroke," she said softly and added with a smile. "As well as sunburn."

He said, "That's your response to my embarrassing confession?"

Rebecca stood up from the chair and slowly padded over to him, holding out her hand. He took it and pulled her down to straddle him.

"That's what I like about you," she said. "You're not afraid to put things into words. Telling me that. You like to speak, don't you?"

"I suppose," he said, with a shrug.

"You know what you should have been?" Rebecca said, leaning in for a kiss as Heslin wished Fred could see what his old lady was up to now.

"What?"

"An actor."

"Piss off."

He pushed her away and she went out to the kitchen, giving him time to think.

What the Hell was it about her?

He should hate her. He should have called her bluff and sodded off but here he was.

God, what had she done to him? Why was his armour coming off? Because she was stunning? Because she needed his help? Needed *him*?

Did he love being *needed* for the first time?

Looking at her as she sashayed back into the room with two large glasses of wine and a smile on her face. Just setting the wine down and moving over to the record player, humming a Neil Young tune – he couldn't remember the title – she oozed sex. She teased without knowing it, she had eyes he could get lost in, a body he couldn't keep his hands off, she was just so... so *bloody* comfortable in her own skin and he couldn't believe she was his.

And when the needle hit the groove and "Walk On" came through the speaker, Rebecca slowly came back to him. Heslin sat up, she passed him his glass, they clinked and kissed.

"What are you smiling at?" she said.

"Things," he murmured. "The way things change. It's... Never mind."

"Tell me."

"I wanted to say something deep but struggled. Never mind."

Rebecca kissed him and started to laugh.

TEN

Entry & Exit

All I wanted today was to not get beaten up, not run into Jim Mudd, not run into Kidney and not have to see the coppers unless they were gonna tell me they'd found my records safe and sound.

I didn't wanna run into Kelly Mudd again either and, OK, I didn't actually run into her, but I did shoot past her on Scawton Lane. She was waiting to cross, looking very tasty indeed. I would have stopped – just to see how she was and all but she'd crossed that line now. Keith Moran didn't wanna ride the town bike, no sir.

I went north, slowly when a couple of coppers went past then really let her go as I reached the country, hitting eighty by the power station. Then came the steep climb, winding and winding until it was flat again and I could see my town laid out in the valley below, smoke piling into the sky.

It wasn't quite noon yet and my hangover was going slowly. I'd got pissed in front of the telly and ended up watching Bogart escape from – not Alcatraz – but this other prison in San Francisco. Like all the others, he ended up screwing Lauren Bacall and fuck me, was she out of his league. It was alright. The start was all from his viewpoint and that got annoying but last night I only wanted to watch something where I didn't have to think.

It was so quiet up here that if the view hadn't been smoggy, I'd have stayed there, laid in the grass, watching life go by down below. A telescope, a few cans and a bird. Maybe I should have stopped when I saw Kelly.

Turning around, I took the road into the woods reaching the meeting point – the crossroads slap bang in the centre – and there I stopped, propping the bike against the tree.

I was throwing up and thinking about another free Chinky when I heard the Scimitar behind me, screeching round the corner and getting to about sixty. The crazy bitch braked hard, skidmarks in the road behind her and stuck her bony face out of the window when they reached me.

"Good afternoon, Keith," she said.

"Hiya."

Luke leant across her to shake my hand, massive, poser's shades on his face.

I had to be fake with him now.

"Hide your bike and get in," Rebecca said. "We're going for a drive."

Hide my bike, I thought. Something else for the bastards to nick if they find it. I pushed it into a ditch behind the sign and pulled some brambles and stuff over it.

"You've got the plans?"

I patted my pocket and told Luke I was sitting in the front. *Told* him.

"'Clunk, click, every trip,' Keith. Tell him how I drive, Luke."

"Like a dervish," he said, pulling my seat back into place.

I didn't know what one of those was. Rebecca burned off, smile on her face, enjoying herself. She'd have had the roof down if she could. Turning to Luke, he raised his eyebrows. It was a bloke thing that meant we didn't have to say anything, we just *knew*.

But I knew other stuff now too.

"Get your job back?" I asked.

"Did I Hell," he said over the engine. "They've bloody replaced me. Told me I'll never work in that town again. Bastards."

"I told you, you should have punched him like that bloke from the sheet metal foundry did."

"Yeah, well," he said with a shrug, looking out the window. "I still might."

"They might make a film about this one day. I don't know who'd be me. Who'd be you?"

"I would," he said, and sounded serious.

"Where we going? Back to yours?"

Rebecca shook her head, staring at the road.

"Where then?"

"We're getting a look at Browning's from up high."

Luke murmured something about this being the third time this week and she blew him a kiss in the mirror.

When we came out of the woods, she pulled onto a verge with the factory below on the left. Again, a cracking view if it wasn't for the smoke. Browning should have sold up. He'd have got a right packet for that land. Nice little housing estate outside town instead of a crap pile.

Rebecca handed me the binos and I went out for a better look. Luke got out too, standing beside me and asking for the plans.

It took him a while to spread them on the ground. "How do we get in?"

"Through the front gate."

"Really? Not over the wall?"

"Nah," I said. "We walk up the drive bang on half three."

"Why then?"

"Cos that's when Terry goes for his walk. We sort out Cheesey at the gate. Club him a couple of times."

"I don't wanna sound like the wet blanket but…"

"No, he won't die. Not if you hit him in the right place. Here," I said, touching my neck, watching three lorries being loaded down below.

"What about guard dogs?"

"None."

"Who's Cheesey?"

"Frank Cheese."

"Then what? God, I need a drink."

"When he's done, we need a distraction. A brick through one of them windows or something to get Terry to come look. Again, same treatment. Leave him somewhere."

"Drag him back to the gate, yeah? Leave them together?"

I put the binos down and turned to him. "We stick him in the yard. You take his keys and get us in through that door there."

He took the binos. "Which door?"

"The red one below ground level. Here, you're looking in the wrong…"

"Got it. Right. Where does that lead?"

"Here." I knelt beside the plan, a massive sheet of white paper, covered in black lines. They'd drawn it for

Aldo because he kept getting lost. "Two areas. Production. Distribution. Both on the ground level. You see where them lorries are now? That's Distribution on the left. They make it in this room, stick it in cans round the back then it ends up on shelves in Distribution. This drawing's simple. There's more to it than that."

"Is this ground level?"

"No, listen, I already said it were below ground. This is where we go in and this is where we start the fire. Right before we get here. Top right. The top floor, floor four. There."

I pointed to the far right corner.

"Yeah, I meant to ask you about that. That gap between the door and the smokestack. Why's that there?"

"There used to be a walkway. You can't see it but there's rungs on that stack going right to the top. They go down too and we end up in that glass place. That's our escape."

"You're joking?"

"No, we have to jump. I've seen it up close. It's only a few feet and you get a run up."

"Why don't we go back the way we came?" he said, sounding nervous.

"Cos the fire cuts off our escape. This is the only way out. Through that door, down the smokestack and into the far corner to get over the wall."

"Where the pallets are stacked?"

"Yeah, we're using pallets to get us up the wall. Anyway, you need to know about the offices."

"Top right?" He kept flitting between looking down at the plans and down at the factory. "Don't you need to know this?" he called back to the car.

"I'm listening, movie star. You boys play nicely now."

"Four offices side-by-side. Far corner, Browning's. Next is his secretary."

"What's she like?"

"Dirty. Personnel and then Payroll."

"We need to be in Payroll?"

"Yeah. There's a massive safe mounted in the wall full of our lovely money."

"He pays in cash?"

"Course he pays in cash. It's easier."

"Hang on," Luke said. "I need to water the horse." He crossed over the road and went into the trees, unzipping his fly before he'd even got there.

"Keith, come here," Rebecca called from the car.

I stuck my head in.

She was laid back in her seat, bare feet on the dashboard and with those big shades over her eyes, looked scary when she lifted her head up. "Are you alright?" she said softly.

"Yeah. I think."

"I enjoyed our walk round the lake."

"Yeah," I said, seeing Luke crossing back over. "Me too."

"Good boy."

Luke was looking through the binos again, scratching his chest. "You got any booze in the car?" he shouted.

"No," she said.

"You coming, Keith?"

"Go on then," Rebecca said, smiling. "Get back to playing army."

"How do we get the safe open?" Luke was asking as I strolled back.

"This is the genius part. In fact, this is so stupid that I can't believe Browning's not been robbed before. Everyone in the factory, everyone in the *Collier's* knows this. Cheesey has the first three numbers. Terry the second three. If they wanted, they could empty that safe and piss off to Argentina."

"How do they have them? Paper? Or is it stored up here? And why would they need those numbers? Are you sure about this? It sounds like bullshit."

"Cos they change the code every Saturday evening after the day shift knock off. Browning changes it. Terry or Cheesey witnesses the first three numbers and the other the second. Browning probably thinks they don't share the numbers. He's so stupid but they're like brothers them two. For all we know, they might help themselves to a few quid every Saturday when there's no-one around."

"They'll keep books, Keith. Every penny'll be accounted for. How do we get the code?"

"We beat it out of 'em."

"How big are these geezers?"

"Cheesey's about your size but probably can't handle himself as well as you. Terry's bigger but softer. So what? There'll be two of us and we'll have tools. We burst in on Cheesey, ask for the safe code and whether he gives it to us or not, smack him across the knees with the wrench. And again until he realises that the only way he can walk for the rest of his life is to give us what we want. Then over the head with the same wrench and we're in. Cheesey'd better know all six numbers. He'll wish he did. If not, Terry ends up in the wheelchair too."

"Tell me something bad about these two geezers so I'll find it easier to belt them."

"Erm... They're alright blokes actually. Terry bought me a couple of pints on me nineteenth."

"Great."

"Cheesey probably hits the missus when he's had a bad shift."

"We should probably break his fingers then."

"Can do."

"That was a joke, Keith." Luke shook his head and thrust his hands in his pockets. "Where are you in all this?" he called back to her.

"I'm the wheels man," she said.

He pointed to the smokestack after a while of heavy breathing. "What if that door doesn't open?"

"We break it down."

"And fall out the other side? Four storeys."

"Why are you...?"

"Because I've got more to lose than you," he snapped. "If I get nicked breaking into that dump, the bloody press'll have a field day. Let's ignore the police for a second. I get arrested – everyone'll ask why a man off the telly is spending his Saturday nights burning paint vats."

"They're not vats, they're..."

"And what's my defence? I needed the money. 'Why, doesn't acting pay?' 'No your honour, not when you've been blacklisted.' Or do I tell them I've...?" He looked over to the Scimitar to see Rebecca coming to join us. "Do I tell them I met someone who made... asked me to do it for her?"

I looked from him to her and she looked like she was right in love with him – the kinda look Kelly used to give me before *and* after but never during.

This wasn't making sense to me.

It went against what I knew and I felt like I was intruding.

She walked up behind him and put her arms around his waist, nestling her head against his back.

For the first time that day I was aware of the noises of nature around us. Birds above and all that crap. Christ, I didn't even know where to stand.

"I never meant for it to happen," Luke murmured. "It just did. Sometime between Monday and today."

He turned back to face her and they looked into each others' eyes like Bogart and Bacall from last night.

"There's a coincidence," she said and they started kissing like I wasn't around.

I grabbed my plans and went back to the Scimitar, leaning on the bonnet to study them. OK, I wasn't really studying them – I just wanted somewhere else to look.

"Keith, come here," Luke said when they'd finished rubbing my face in their *passion*. "I'm sorry for being a prick just now. This is all new to me, that's all."

"It's new to all of us." Rebecca said. "He's not a criminal either."

"I know, I know. You've done a bang up job of planning this mate, really you have and I didn't mean I had more to lose if it turns to custard. I only meant I'd lose everything more publicly. Imagine how you'd react if Rodney Bewes was on the front page of *The Sun* for criminal damage or something."

"Bob Ferris banged up? Thelma'd go mental."

"Bolam I could believe," Rebecca said, taking her shades off.

Luke put his arms around her.

"We're all in this together," she said. "We're all going down if it goes wrong and we all have to keep our wits about us to make sure it doesn't. In forty-eight hours we'll be financially secure..."

"Fuck me, where did you get that from? 'Financially secure?' You mean *rich*," I said.

"Luke and I can retire to Bordeaux, and Keith, you can afford to get your hair cut."

"For the last fuckin' time," I said, "I'm growing it. Like Bowie."

Luke was too busy feeling the sun on his face and thinking about booze to see his woman wink at me with that huge grin on her face.

ELEVEN

Keith

When they asked this old soldier how he got by, living with what he did, all he said was, "You know it's coming, you know it's gonna be tough and you know you'll be a changed man afterwards but you just get on and do it. Don't think about it too much beforehand, definitely don't think about it while you're doing it and do your best to forget it afterwards."

He reckoned that's what had kept him sane since the war:

It's coming.

It's happening.

It happened.

End of.

"Like popping your cherry," he said afterwards, and you could hear him laughing, "but without the whisky for your nerves."

It was around eight o'clock Saturday night and I was eating ham sarnies by the slurry pits where Joan Hurst drowned.

God, if my mam could see me, she'd have a fit.

Growing up, just me and her, she'd always been on about me keeping safe, staying off train tracks, crossing the road and hanging round the pits outside of town. Maybe she should have got Fred Dryden and Joan Hurst in a room together and warned them both.

God, if my mam could know what I was about to do now, she'd have an even bigger fit.

But I reckon if my mam was still around, I wouldn't be in this state, wouldn't be thinking about the thing I wasn't meant to be thinking about. Wouldn't have been burgled living at my mam's. She'd have flattened Jim Mudd for laying his hands on me. Would have gated me for going anywhere near the Plough.

"That Rebecca," she'd have said, "She's a wrong 'un."

She'd be right. Rebecca was a wrong 'un but give her her due mam, all she wanted was to live in sin with her bloke. It wasn't like *she'd* run him over. We'd have argued about that.

I was smiling as I finished my sarnies and threw the crusts in the slurry.

What else wouldn't she like? Christ, this could take all night.

Robbery for a start.

Arson.

Getting rich off others' backs.

My swearing.

She wouldn't think it right Rebecca approaching me that time we met – would think it too forward even though we were just mates. The bike – she'd hate that. The Bowie cut – that would have to go. Kelly Mudd – God, if my mam knew about her and that waiter – she'd go off like that bomb the Indians exploded last May.

My records – she'd have liked most of them. The soul stuff, Motown, all that. They played Percy Sledge at her funeral and yeah, the words didn't fit because no man but me ever loved my mam but it was her favourite and it sounded great in church. She liked a dance, loved Smokey Robinson voice, reckoned she could have been a Supreme if she'd been in the right place at the right time. That's a pretty big fucking *if* though mam and I'm sorry for swearing.

If I'd been in the right place at the right time I'd… Who knows? But tonight, OK so I was nervous, but I was definitely in the right place at the right time.

Half a mile away I could see Browning's, the three chimneys – chimleys my mam'd call them – spewing smoke into the evening sky.

I stood up and stretched.

It was time to do what Bogart'd call 'casing'. Time to 'case the joint'. I knew it inside out but a final walk round the walls on this side – checking nothing could prevent a clean getaway – wouldn't harm me.

Unless I got seen.

But – and I don't get this – that was part of the thrill.

Stashing everything in my bag, I wheeled my bike further down the track and into the undergrowth down the bank, pulling branches and stuff over it best I could. Then I moved on, heading for the pipe crossing the slurry pit that Joan had fallen off when Paul Oldham was chasing her for a laugh.

Arms out, I made it across no problem and headed down towards the line of trees flanking the ditch a few hundred metres away. With them giving cover, I moved parallel towards the back of the factory, seven hundred yards or so to my right.

It was around half eight now and they knocked off at that time on Saturday night, all piling into town for a swift half in the Collier's then home for a bath and straight back out – heading down the Malt Shovel, the Three Tuns, the Boot, the Rising Sun, the Tramway, the Railway & Bicycle then onto the Visage for a drink, a dance, a fag and a shag.

Everyone lives for Saturday nights, I thought, as I broke cover and ran across the field for the high red brick wall. Saturday night was what kept us all going. It was my mam's dominoes night at the Horseshoe.

Keith, stop thinking about your mam. It was trying not to think about the other thing that was making her creep into my mind. Sorry mam. Sorry for what I'm about to do but my records got nicked, I'm running low on money and it is dog eat dog out there. Plus Browning's a bastard.

Getting to the wall, I put my back up to it and looked right up as windows on the floors above were being closed.

Cheesey and Terry came on at night and Browning always went out to chat to them at the gate before he went home in his TR6 and got through a bottle of Haig's and a packet of Cubans watching *Parkinson* and passing out in his armchair. I smiled. That's where he'd be when he got the call telling him his pride and joy was up in flames.

I moved along the wall and reached the corner, where, on the other side, the pallets were stacked. It was about a fifteen foot drop down this side but the ground was soft enough. Fuck it, if I did break my ankle, I could pay cash to have it fixed up in no time anyway.

Looking up, I could see that lonely smokestack I was gonna escape onto and panicked, thinking, what if we can't get that door open?

And panicked again, thinking, what if it all goes to pot?

What if they don't give us the code?

What if the safe's been moved?

What if we just can't get in?

Panicking about all that crap now. I'd been panicking over it for three weeks now and every time she'd been there to tell me it'd be alright, tell me she'd done her reading, done her spying and all that.

So stop panicking yourself, Keith, it's gonna be fine. Aldo gave you the floorplan. You've been in Payroll before. You've even seen the safe get opened. Six numbers and you've got the wages of five hundred people to spend.

I was feeling my way along the wall now, towards the entrance, where the side of the building stopped and became a wire fence. I could hear cars starting up, horns beeping as the workers piled out. I could hear them talking, dying to get that stink out of their nostrils, dig out their flares and kippers and hit the dancefloor. Then Sunday morning – sleeping hangovers off and starting again at dinnertime.

Dropping to one knee, avoiding the sheet of plate glass some dickhead had left there, I shifted round to look through the fence at them walking away from me, all their backs familiar.

And you know what I thought?

Fuck them all.

Good lads, most of them, yeah. But fuck them for not having my balls to do this, to take a risk and fuck them for not being lucky enough to have a skinny Jane Seymour lookalike take a shine to them and let them in on her little secret. That was it. That's who she looked like. Jane Seymour but paler. Like Jane Seymour if she had what my mam had.

I backed away for a rest, laying down in the dirt and looking up at the darkening sky and thinking about Rebecca. Thinking about her face when I got in that Scimitar and upended my bag and notes dropped out. And OK, so she'd been into Luke but I reckon she'd show me how grateful she could be. Not my type, I liked them with curves, but any hole's a goal and she wasn't the shy type when she'd had a drink. She looked the shy type, quite prudish, but looks are deceiving, aren't they?

Rebecca looked like a frigid children's nurse but she'd gone backstage at that Faces gig after too much gin and ended up having herself a real good time.

I smiled, remembering her telling me that, sitting on my couch pissed and giggly then driving home – wherever that was – hammered. The coppers would never pull her over, no sir. A woman driving an orange Reliant Scimitar at three hundred miles an hour? They'd think, fuck it, she's the type knows her rights, let's let her be.

And Luke? He looked like Robert Redford, a man the ladies liked, but from what I'd seen and heard, he wasn't that type at all.

As for me, I was looking more like Bowie every day, but what was I doing right now? Casing the joint for the most important night of my life.

I was thinking too much.

That's where all these random thoughts were coming from. I was trying too hard to not think about what was coming. You couldn't not think though, could you? I bet that old soldier thought about other stuff to keep the wolf from the door. Your mind's not like a refrigerator, is it? You can't just empty it. There's always stuff in there.

119

I wondered what he thought about when he wasn't thinking about killing Jerries. I wondered what I'd think about when I didn't have to worry about money. When I didn't have to worry about anything. What did rich people think about?

I sat up and crawled back to the fence in time to see Cheesey coming up towards the gatehouse, walking like John Wayne.

He went straight in – I could see through the window – put his bag on the side and shook hands with Leon and Groomy then folded his arms and started one of his stories.

Where Terry was, I didn't know. They always came together, sometimes had a kickabout in the yard during the week. I'd seen them out the window once at two in the morning, floodlit and pissing it down, but they didn't care.

Cheesey wrapped his story up with a headbutt and Leon and Groomy were still pissing themselves when Browning crossed the yard and went into the gatehouse. They stopped laughing and Cheesey shook Browning's hand that bit too much, probably thanking him for not selling up.

Browning nodded and Groomy joined in the praise.

Dog eat dog, gents, I thought. Not dog lick other dog's balls.

Cheesey folded his arms as Browning said something. Cheesey nodded and Leon and Groomy left as Browning checked his watch.

I watched them duck under the barrier and walk away and strained to see another bloke coming up to them in the security uniform. Because of the barrier I couldn't make out his face when they stopped to chat, and a second later, Browning and Cheesey stepped out and were coming towards me, Browning talking with his hands.

I quickly moved backwards, still crouching.

Losing my balance, my foot went right through the plate glass and it shattered, making the loudest noise ever.

Cheesey and Browning stopped and looked around, their eyes in the wrong direction but sweeping quickly towards me.

I didn't wait around.

I went full height, turned and ran proper quickly along the wall, deliberately kicking up dust behind me so they couldn't get a glance.

Reaching the end of the wall, I ducked round the corner, got my breath and ran full pelt for the trees, cursing the dickhead who'd left the glass there.

What had my little recce achieved?

Nothing, other than nearly being spotted.

But as long as the inside of Browning's hadn't changed, we were fine, because the outside was still exactly the same.

Checking my watch, I realised that for all of one hour and eleven minutes I hadn't thought about the thing at all.

And for that, I was gonna roar off into town for a pint in the Horseshoe, in memory of my mam, before kick off in six hours.

Twelve

The Smokestack

Heslin didn't give a damn about Turkey, Cyprus or Richard Nixon – he'd only had the wireless on before coming out to take his mind off this.

Rebecca had filled him with coffee and given him four bottles of Smirnoff, several cloths and matches before they got in the Scimitar at three in the morning and sped off – Rebecca driving in her underwear because it turned them on.

It was a minor criminal blip, that's all it was. Once it was out of the way, he had his whole life to be who he was with her. Together in foreign climes and all the screwing on the beach he could manage.

That's what he kept telling himself.

At three twenty, they sped over the bridge at Ryeford, pulling in at the end. She turned the engine off and kissed him. "Close your eyes," she said.

When he did he felt her tights go over his head and she laughed. Heslin flicked the light on and got a look in the wing mirror. Screw it – he could intimidate anyone like this because he looked like a proper villain. A real hard case.

"Here," Rebecca said, opening the glove compartment.

The handcuffs and gaffer tape dropped out and he caught them.

He could hear Keith's motorbike in the distance and as it came into view, he noticed she --was looking at him in that way again.

"Luke," she said.

"Keith's gonna see your knickers," he said, pulling the tights off his head.

"Luke."

"What?"

She took his face between her hands and kissed him harder than before, like she'd never stop. As the beam from Keith's bike shone in his eyes, she leant into his ear. "Thank you for doing this for us," she whispered. "I'll never ever forget it."

Heslin smiled at her and took the bag from his feet, dropping the tights and handcuffs into it. He got out and nodded to Keith.

"Got everything?"

"Yeah. You?"

"Yeah."

"Pick me up here at seven, you," Heslin said to Rebecca.

He climbed up behind Keith and she blew him a kiss, telling him not to drink the vodka. They moved off, hearing her start the Scimitar and turn back onto the bridge.

It was two miles of flat country road to Browning's, Heslin getting that mixture of stage fright and adrenaline, that buzz he loved about performing. Blimey, this must be the *The Crucible* of criminal activity, he thought with the wind in his hair, *Hamlet* even.

The bike soon slewed to a halt and Keith skidded, sending gravel flying into the ditch.

"Get off," he said. "I'm gonna stick her down there."

He pointed to a dip in the field to the right of the factory, illuminated by the moonlight. Heslin climbed down into the ditch as Keith wheeled the bike, returning ten minutes later.

Simultaneously they pulled their masks – tights and balaclava helmet – on and simultaneously they started laughing, Keith sounding more nervous than Heslin.

"An hour until wealth," Heslin said. "Let's move. What?"

"What?"

"Why are you staring at me?"

"I weren't."

Pulling their gloves on, they walked stealthily up the long straight road to the gatehouse, Keith in front. When they were thirty feet away, they crouched and Keith pulled a monkey wrench from his coat.

"Here," he said, tossing a flick knife to Heslin.

Keith ducked under the barrier and crept to the door. Heslin followed slower, one hand firmly on the bag to stop the bottles clinking. They pressed their backs against the wall, hearing some student on the wireless phone-in inside, boring the county with his views on inflation.

"Let's do it," Keith hissed.

Heslin got a final rush and a final *no turning back* as Keith burst through the gatehouse door.

The security guard turned round, eyes wide, hand shooting to the radio but Keith beating him to it and bringing the wrench down. The radio shattered, the remnants hitting the floor.

"Bloody Hell," he said. "Couple of hard bastards, eh?"

As he went to stand up, Keith swung the wrench at his cheek, Heslin hearing a crack as the bloke went from his chair and into the wall.

On instinct, Heslin flicked the knife open and reached for a pair of handcuffs. "You don't wanna get hit again, you'll bloody well roll onto your fat belly and stick your hands behind your back, yeah?"

"You're kidding," he laughed. "A tool and a knife and you think you can take me? Where's your shooters?"

Keith ran over to him and went to boot his face but the guard grabbed his ankle, twisted it and pushed him across the room. Keith smacked onto the bank of desks, spun round and grabbed the wireless, throwing it hard. It landed on the guard's nose, the student shut up, the nose burst and Heslin was on the guard's back, knife to his throat, promising to slice the jugular if the bastard didn't get on his bloody knees and play nicely.

The guard went down, shaking his head, knife biting into his neck.

"Cuff him," Heslin said.

Keith got up and manoeuvred himself between them, snapping the cuffs on the guard's wrists.

Heslin released the knife. "Code for the safe. Give it to us."

"I don't have it."

"Yes you do. We know you do."

"Not all of it."

"Don't be a dickhead, Cheesey," Keith said. "Yeah, that's right, we know who you are, Frank Cheese. You don't know us but we know you. Browning gives you the last three numbers and Terry the others. But you share 'em in case you have moments like this, y'know, when you know if you don't hand the code over you lose your kneecaps."

Cheesey was shaking his head, smiling.

Heslin thought, was this how all these things started? A hero giving you no choice but to hurt him?

"This is your first time, isn't it?" Cheesey said. "You, you're a kid and you, you're a bit older. I'd say twenty and twenty-six. One or both of you work here, I can tell that. You," he said, staring at Keith. "I'd recognise you without the balaclava on. You, yeah, I'll know you the next time I see you."

"Shut up and give us the code."

"Oh I will, don't worry. I'll give you all six numbers. But first, I'll give you something else. A little warning." He sighed, laughed and shook his head. "When you're gone from here, get as far away as you can. For your sake, please don't ever come back to town. Don't think about coming back here."

He looked Heslin full in the face, Heslin starting to feel naked under the itching tights.

"I know people," he said slowly. "I know *people*. Do you understand?"

Sweat ran down Heslin's spine.

"A couple of blows with a wrench and sitting here till the coppers turn up and letting Browning's wages blow away are absolutely nothing compared to what's gonna happen to you when this is over. I'll see you both again, maybe not till eighty or ninety-five but I'll see you. You want the code? Here. Twenty-two. Twelve. Forty-four. Twenty-three. Fifty-two. Seventy-seven. Get that?"

Keith wrote it on Cheesey's *Telegraph* and tore the page out.

"Good luck," Cheesey grinned.

Heslin turned the lights off after Keith had wrapped gaffer tape round Cheesey's mouth and smashed the telephone. They walked out into the yard.

"That didn't go well," Heslin muttered.

"He were talking out of his arse," Keith said. "We got the code, didn't we?"

"No we didn't. He made those numbers up. Let's find the other one."

They crossed to the red door. Heslin picked up an empty paint tin and threw it through one of the windows. At that time it sounded like the loudest noise in the world. They waited several minutes before Keith shrugged. "He didn't hear. Come on. Let's get on with it." He booted the door.

"No," Heslin hissed. "We need to take care of the other one first. If he finds his mate like that, we're screwed. We'll have all the police in the county on our arse."

They glared at each other in the moonlight.

"Break another window."

Keith handed him a torch from his inside pocket and Heslin shone it around, seeing nothing he could throw.

"Come on, Luke. Here, you wait here and if he turns up, sort him out. I'll have a look inside."

He booted the door again and as it began to splinter, Heslin grabbed his shoulder, squeezing hard. "Good idea, mate. But if we're splitting up, I want the code on me."

"Eh? You've got it. You heard him."

"I can't remember, now give it to me."

"How do you remember your lines?"

"Because they're words not numbers."

"You think I'm gonna run off? Christ, Luke, grow up. We're in this together, OK?"

"Why do you keep staring at me then?"

"You what? What you talking about?"

"You know what," Heslin murmured.

They stood in near-silence, their heavy breathing all Heslin could hear. He shook his head. "I've noticed," he said after a while.

"Noticed?"

"The way you look at her. Don't think that…"

Keith shoved him into the wall and Heslin responded with a punch to the guts, sinking Keith to his knees.

"Christ, Luke, what were…? I don't…"

Heslin grabbed his shoulders and hauled him up. "You're a good lad, Keith. But don't try and ruin this for me. Gimme the paper."

Panting, Keith handed the paper over, shaking his head before shouldering the door and stepping inside.

Heslin crossed the yard back to the gatehouse, walking right back in and ignoring Cheesey mouthing some bullshit behind his gag. He grabbed a chair from the corner and went back out, running across the yard and hurling it against a window. It bounced off the frame and he was picking it up when he heard his name called from inside.

Heslin dropped the chair and plunged down the steps, his torch shining the way.

"Help me!"

Keith was up ahead, being strangled by the other guard and bloody Hell his balaclava was off. It lay on the floor by his torch. Jesus…

The guard pulled Keith's hair and dragged him over to a work bench, ready to bring his head down on a vice when Heslin leapt on him, sending them both crashing to the floor. Heslin dropped the torch and couldn't find his knife as two hands closed on his neck.

"He crept up on me," Keith hissed.

Heslin and the guard rolled over, Heslin taking a couple of blows to the face and his burnt chest stinging like nobody's business. He caught the guard's wrists, rolled so he was on top and headbutted him on the nose. The guard fell back but came straight back up until Heslin and Keith landed blows on his head simultaneously.

He was out of it.

Heslin slumped to the floor, cross-legged.

Keith staggered back to the work bench and sat with his back to it, panting.

"Luke?"

"What?"

Keith shone the torch on the man laid still. "It's Aldo."

"Oh shit. Did he see your face?"

Keith nodded, looking like he was about to cry.

"Oh my God. Oh my God, I don't believe this."

"What are we gonna do, Luke?"

"I don't know. Keith, if he names you... Please mate, please keep me out of this. You won't get long, a couple of years. We're mates, yeah? Just... take this one for me."

Keith started nodding, his face screwing up. He was gonna cry any second. "What do we do, Luke? What do we do? He jumped me and pulled it off. He said me name. He were surprised, couldn't believe it were me.

Aldo the Eyetie, me mate, and he's there punching me like I were a burglar or something," he sniffed. "Oh Luke, help me, please? I can't go…"

"Shut up."

Heslin shuffled towards Aldo and went to roll him over. He paused, feeling sick. "Shine your light on him."

Aldo's eyes were wide open, unblinking.

He wasn't breathing.

"Luke…"

"You bloody killed him, you little prick!"

"Me…? I…?" Keith said, getting to his feet.

"He's dead, you stupid…"

"I didn't hit him…"

"You clocked him one just then, there. On his head. Jesus, Keith…"

"That were you!"

"You hit him!"

"You… you hit him harder… It were you…"

"No it wasn't!"

"You… you belted him, you smashed him on his head. You broke his nose…"

Heslin put his hands to his mouth, breathing heavily, unable to believe this. This bloody DJ had *murdered*.

He'd killed.

The DJ had done it, Keith, he'd…

Hadn't he?

"It were you, Luke," Keith said quietly. "I barely touched him."

"Piss off, I had it under control, you didn't have to biff him."

"Luke, mate, honestly…"

"Don't *honestly* me, Keith. Don't bloody well speak to me like that, you little murdering…"

"It weren't me!"

Heslin swung for him, connecting with his left eye, Keith collapsing without a fight. Heslin booted him four times in the ribs then stopped mid-kick as Keith tried squirming away.

"Alright," Heslin said, out of breath. "Sod it."

"You what?"

"He's dead, yeah? It doesn't matter how or why now."

"He were me mate," Keith said, tears in his eyes, rubbing his ribs. "Why would I kill him?"

"Because he knew you. Jesus, what a mess. Get up."

Keith sniffed and got to his feet. "What do we do?"

"Leave him here," Heslin said, looking at the dead Italian on the floor and feeling further from *Motown Cop* than ever. "We let him burn."

"He had a kid on the way…"

"So what?" Heslin snapped. "Tough shit, alright? He was… unlucky."

"Sorry Aldo," Keith murmured. "Two in one night."

"Gimme the plans."

With tears in his eyes, Keith reached into his back pocket and handed them over. Heslin spread them on the floor. "It's those stairs we take? Over there?"

"Yeah."

"You're a pussy, Keith. You know that?"

"Fuck off," he almost sobbed. "If it had been you he'd seen you'd…"

"What's he even doing here? You said he was a foreman."

"You get paid more for this. Maybe Terry had a night off."

"Here," Heslin said, handing him his bag. "Burn it. Yeah? We'll have time, won't we?"

Keith nodded. "It's four flights and we're there. Jump, down, up and over into the field. Oh Christ, Luke, what am I gonna do?"

"You're gonna run like bloody Cruyff once we're back at the bridge. You're gonna... Why are you looking at me like that? What are you smiling for?"

"Nothing."

"Tell me."

"It's... You're a real mate, Luke. And I'm sorry I let you down."

Heslin sighed – glad tights were harder to pull off a head than a balaclava.

They had a few moments breathing time.

Heslin said, "Meet me at the top of the stairs. You know where the combustible stuff is?"

"Next door mostly."

"Then set that going."

Heslin took a torch and hurried to the doors in the far corner, going up all four flights and gagging on the smell of disinfectant. That bleeding stupid DJ. So cocky yesterday with his know-all attitude. Three weeks to plan this and he'd fallen at the first hurdle, the useless murdering bastard.

God knows what she'd say.

At the top, Heslin peered out at the moon and down at that greenhouse and got that panic from the telephone box again. Oh shit, he was going down for a very long time unless something bloody miraculous happened.

How fast could that Scimitar get them to Bordeaux?

Before Frank Cheese tells the Regional Crime Squad suits gathered round his hospital bed that Keith Moran belted him?

Before Keith Moran collapses under bright lights from hourly beatings in that police station and blames the Redford lookalike for killing the Italian?

Before he says the actor did the worst stuff?

And not just the actor but the woman with the dark eyes who organised this because Browning ran her boyfriend over?

Because the woman thought, sod it, if I'm gonna get revenge, I'm gonna get rich too.

Heslin could have smiled. No car could move faster than all that, no matter what its bleeding horsepower.

Four floors below he heard smashing noises seconds apart.

Maybe it was better Aldo had died. If not, he'd have named Keith and... Keith killing Aldo had bought them more time.

Oh shit, Luke, he thought, when did you become so immune?

A door burst open below and he could hear Keith running up the stairs. A heatwave hit him a few moments later, Keith rubbing his back, his balaclava back on.

"What's...?"

"I dropped the last bottle right below us. When it takes hold – boom – these floors'll collapse. No trace of anything we do up here."

"Please tell me you let the other three off..."

"Two in Distribution, the other in Production. This place is swimming in toxic fumes. Two women fainted last summer cos of 'em. The vodka's like the matches, the paint's the…"

"Alright. You've calmed down?"

"Yeah."

"It'll be alright, Keith. Whatever your cut, you use it to get as far away from this town as possible. It's only arson."

"Will Browning still go down for this?"

Heslin said, "You run far enough, Keith, and when you open your *Daily Mirror* one morning to see Norman Browning being shoved in the back of a prison van, you might even be grateful you killed Aldo."

They pushed through the double door, Keith spitting on Browning's name plate and Heslin booting the door in to Payroll. He spied the safe set in the far wall, one of the old ones, not very *Motown Cop*.

"What do we do? Just twist that knob?"

"We'll find out. Jesus, smell that."

Fire and chemicals below were making a potent mix. Heslin read out the first number. Keith twisted the dial to twenty-two.

It clicked.

They smiled at each other.

"Twelve."

Dial.

Click.

"He weren't lying."

"Forty-four."

Dial.

Click.

"Twenty-three."

Dial.

Click.

Heslin grinned. Couldn't help it. All that stress and panic was about to pay off.

"Fifty-two."

Dial.

Click.

"Why'd he tell us the truth so quick?"

"I don't know. Seventy-seven."

Dial.

Nothing.

They looked at each other.

"Try again."

Seventy-seven dialled.

Nothing.

"Shit," Heslin hissed. "Let me try."

Seventy-seven dialled.

Nothing.

"Maybe we misheard him."

"Both of us?"

"It could have been twenty-seven?"

"Try it."

Twenty-seven dialled.

Nothing.

Heslin slammed his fist onto the safe. He punched and kicked it. Then he turned on Keith and grabbed his lapels.

"Get over there now and beat it out of him. Kneecaps, ribs, cheekbones, whatever it takes."

"How?"

"Do it!"

"How, Luke? There's only one way out."

"What do you mean?"

"We're trapped. Them stairs lead down into fire. This whole place is gonna – smell that, smell *it*."

Heslin looked out the window. "You'll have to jump. Get down that smokestack and bleeding shout the number…"

A loud rumbling noise from downstairs reached them. Terrifyingly loud. Something collapsed and windows could be heard blowing out.

"What do we do?"

"Try all the sevens. Do it."

Seven dialled.

Nothing.

"Seventeen too?"

"The ones that end in seven? That sound like seven?"

Eleven dialled.

Nothing.

Thirty-seven dialled.

Nothing.

More rumbling, more crashing.

Forty-seven dialled.

Nothing.

Fifty-seven dialled.

Nothing.

Heslin touched his burnt chest, drenched in sweat, heart pounding.

Sixty-seven dialled.

An explosion four floors down.

Nothing.

"Hurry up, Keith. We've tried seventy-seven. Come on."

Eighty-seven dialled.

Metal hitting metal, crashing, rumbling.

Nothing.

Heslin and Keith stared at each other.

"If it's not this, we're…"

Heslin shut up, unable to believe it. So close and…

Sirens.

"Last chance. Ninety-seven."

Dialled.

Nothing.

Heslin booted the safe several times as the room got warmer and the sirens louder.

"Why would he give us five numbers?"

"Playing with us, the bastard."

"I can still do it, let me."

"Let's go, Keith."

Keith was fiddling with the dial when Heslin grabbed his shoulders and shoved him to the door. "Where's the exit? Which door?"

"I can't…"

"Which door, Keith? Sod the money, let's get out of here."

He could get a new agent, one who'd stand up to Sidney King and his firm, a pushier one who didn't have a mouse like Melanie taking his calls. He'd tried crime, now it was back to the day job at all costs.

Keith pointed to the door, hidden behind a filing cabinet.

Heslin looked out of the front window at a swarm of pandas tearing up the road towards the gates – three fire engines following.

Then he got his shoulder behind the cabinet – ignoring Keith muttering something – and they slid it out of the way.

Three kicks on the lock and the door swung open, off its hinges and down, through the greenhouse below.

"Far corner, pallets, yeah?" Heslin said.

Keith ignored him and backed off for a run up just as the front barrier went up and the police pulled in. Then Keith was out through the door, over the gap and clutching the rungs of the ladder, climbing *upwards*.

"What are you doing? Oh Jesus," Heslin said, looking down.

Dizziness, vertigo and blind panic swept over him.

"I don't... I can't..."

"You'll have to. It's nothing. Don't look down. Two minutes and we're free. Look, I'll help you."

Keith was holding on with his right hand, leaning out with his left outstretched. It was this or prison.

The man from *Motown Cop* in the slammer?

Heslin took a run up as firemen poured out of their engines. He moved so bloody fast and leapt out over the abyss, reaching for Keith's hand.

But Keith's hand disappeared and his boot connected with Heslin's face instead.

Heslin had nothing to grab, to hold, his heart exploding with terror as he hit the wall and fell.

He plunged eighty feet down and through the glass roof, hitting that concrete floor – minor criminal blip over forever – *knowing* he'd been murdered but not knowing why.

THIRTEEN

The Getaway

So that was it.

No richer than I went in.

OK, she'd have her revenge but neither of us would get a penny. But neither would that double-crossing bastard who wanted me dead.

I landed in a soft clump of deep grass and started running across to where the bike lay, thinking, should I get to Ryeford Bridge and wait for her? Or get straight home and let her contact me? God, she was gonna flip out but what could she do?

I found the bike no problem and wheeled it across to the edge of the woods where I sat tight, watching the factory burn.

She could do everything. Anonymous call to the coppers – drop me right in it – if that's how she felt.

Or maybe she'd understand when I told her we'd got as far as the safe and were only one number out.

Maybe she'd take me abroad with her.

No more Luke Heslin.

Fuck it, now this could be pinned on him. Browning paid an out of work actor to fake a robbery and destroy it for the insurance. Only the bastard got carried away and beat the foreman to death.

Imagine that on the front of *The Sun, Lucas*.

And fuck what he'd said. It wasn't me who killed Aldo. I barely touched him and Luke got what he deserved for killing my mate. That was me in the clear.

I hadn't felt like me in days.

Everything I'd done this last week, everything since meeting her hadn't been like me at all.

Maybe I was punch drunk from all the beatings I'd been given. Yeah, that was it. I was punch drunk and that's why I was sitting in some trees at five in the morning as the sun came up watching a right bonfire.

Grabbing the bike, I pushed it down a narrow path for about a mile through the woods, turning to see if I was being followed every few minutes. When I got to the other side, I sped off towards Ryeford to see if she was waiting.

No sign but then I was an hour early.

Stashing the bike under the bridge, I took a piss by some bushes and was wandering over the bridge when I heard sirens from the far side.

Nowhere to go but down.

I leapt over the railings and plunged into the deep green water, feeling it in my mouth, my nose, my ears, my eyes until I broke the surface, shivering, wiping my Bowie cut back and swimming for the bank. She might laugh when she saw me, all damp and stinking.

Hauling myself up, I saw two pandas in the distance, heading for the factory.

The bells at Ryeford church tolled at seven as I sat shivering in the grass, my clothes draped over the branches of a bush.

Where was she?

She drove in her knickers for fuck's sake. It wasn't like she had to get ready. She'd insisted I shove my bike in the river and I would when she turned up. Not before though. No way was I walking back to town.

I hung around till eight, yawning more and more and knowing I needed to stay awake. All that adrenalin was disappearing and I'd be dead on my feet soon. This was how I felt getting in from Westerton's at dawn, riding past the shift workers, their day beginning and mine ending.

Hurry up, I thought, please just hurry up and get here. I want you to know how close we got and how I covered for us both and how we can be together in another country. She'd have to get a tan and put weight on but I'd poke her in the meantime, why not?

I must have nodded off for a bit, I was that bored.

When I did wake up however long it was later, I yawned, stretched and stood up.

Fuck her, if she wasn't coming, she'd have to get over to mine later for the news. After pulling my damp shirt and jeans on, I pushed the bike up the verge and onto the bridge.

Just in time for another panda coming from the opposite end.

Like when you're at school and you don't wanna be asked a question, I looked down at my bike, pretending there was something wrong with it so they'd speed past.

But they didn't, they crawled up to me and the window went down. "Where you heading, lad?"

"Home."

"Where's home?"

"In town."

"Whereabouts in town?"

"The Picture Palace."

"That street?"

"No," I said. "The actual Picture Palace."

"You live there?"

"A room at the top."

The other one, a WPC, leant over and smiled. "You're the DJ, aren't you? Plays the cricket music at the Visage? Where were you Friday? The records weren't as good."

"I got sacked."

She raised her eyebrows for more.

"Me records got nicked," I said and wanted to cry. I wanted to have a big bawl out and it was nothing to do with Aldo or Luke or this plan going down the toilet. I wanted to cry because my records, the things that made me happy, had been taken from me and these useless coppers hadn't got them back.

"Aw," she said. "How terrible. Did you report it?"

"Last Monday."

"What did we say?"

"The clown on the desk asked me if I had anything by Sparks."

"Well," she began, but he cut in.

"Richardson, I'll handle this. Look, lad," he said. "Who are you, what are you doing here and what's happened to your face?"

"Me face? I... Oh right. I got into a fight on Wednesday. Four of 'em and two... one of me. I reported it."

"I like your bike," the WPC said.

"Thanks."

"What's your name?" from him.

"Keith Moran."

"Keith, I don't know if you've heard or even seen but there were a fire at Mr. Browning's factory in the early hours of this morning. That's where that smoke's coming from."

"What you telling me for?"

"I wondered if you might know anything."

"Why would I?"

"Stop being so defensive," he snapped. "Alright? I'm only asking you a few questions. What are you doing here? Fishing?"

They were both staring at me now and I really wanted to be laid on my bed with Smokey on. Never wanted that so bad in my entire life.

"I were meeting me bird here but she stood me up."

"A girl?"

"Yeah."

"How old is this girl, Keith?"

"What's that got to do with...? Seventeen, alright? She said she wanted to see a sunrise with me," I said, thinking, what a load of shit. "She goes to college next month and that's when September starts and it gets darker so we said we'd do it this weekend but she didn't turn up."

He nodded. He'd bought it. He'd been stood up before. "Keep your eyes peeled, Keith," he said. "It looks bad at Browning's. Deliberate. If you remember seeing anything suspicious then pop along to the station. On your way."

The WPC waved at me as I sped off, head spinning and body dying to be at home. But first, I wanted to get a good look at my handiwork.

By the time I got to the top of the road, a large crowd had gathered at Browning's, watching the smouldering remains of their workplace, smoke spewing up into the sky.

Fifteen hundred unemployed.

Fuck me, they'd lynch the bastard responsible for this when they found him. Providing the coppers didn't check up on me, I'd be in the clear for this, and Browning would be the one with his arse in the noose.

Fire engines sat around and I counted nine pandas and two ambulances. If only I had the binos, I could see if Cheesey was still around.

Cheesey and his promise to find me.

Yeah, good luck.

Around three in the afternoon I was dozing with the radio on, the newsman saying two bodies had been retrieved from the factory.

"The arsonist has been formally identified as one Lucas Heslin, a local man who had been working in London as an actor for some years, who had recently returned home for a holiday."

I turned the radio off and got up.

They'd identified him too soon.

They'd have my name from our arrest.

I grabbed a bag from the top of the wardrobe and flung as many clothes in as I could fit.

The plan?

Get out, fill her up and go all over town to find Rebecca. Ask people if necessary.

It took two minutes to pack.

I blew my room a kiss before stepping out onto the landing.

And there they were.

"Stay there, lad."

Coppers.

Four of them coming in through the door and pounding up the stairs as I set off to the roof.

Oh Christ, I needed to get to my bike.

"Stay!"

I burst through the door and onto the roof, getting a run up and leaping across the alleyway to the roof of the tile merchant, only just making it.

"There he is!"

I dropped my bag and ran across that roof, flat too, and without thinking, took a flying leap onto the roof of another building, lower. Rolling as I landed, I saw two coppers jump from the tile merchant and I was off again.

All of them started blowing their whistles and it proper got my heart pumping.

They weren't far behind as I landed on the roof of the business centre where Kelly worked for six months last year.

Kelly.

I needed Kelly.

Oh shit, out of roofs and they were coming right for me.

The first one had slowed to a walk, his hands up, shaking his head. "Come on, Keith, let's stop this nonsense. We only wanna chat," he said, with the smoke from Browning's behind him.

I turned and ran to the edge, looking down at the street.

Too high to jump.

The copper clocked it at the same time as me.

The telephone pole a few feet from the corner.

Only he was closer to it than me.

The other three landed on the roof and I was trapped. Was I?

I ran and I ran and I ran as fast as I'd ever run and the first one did too, heading to cut me off and for a second I could have stopped and pushed him off but I didn't.

I jumped as he stuck his leg out and I was shooting over the edge, legs out from under me and only just grabbing the pole with both arms.

Splinters plunged into my hands. I cried out and smacked my cheek.

"I said, we only wanna chat, Keith."

"I can't chat if me fuckin' neck's broken, can I?"

I shimmied down as fast as I could, looking up and back to see four thick coppers glaring down at me, the front one with his helmet off, scratching his blond hair.

Pulling out the splinters as I moved, I ran out into the street, a car screeching not to hit me, and then I was into the alleyway between Woolworths and Ekman's Groceries and out the end and across another road and into another alleyway.

Halfway down here, I ducked behind the bins to get my breath back and waited five minutes, praying that Scimitar would arrive with a full tank – Rebecca in bra and driving gloves with a map of Spain or wherever covering her fanny.

No such luck.

I turned right at the end onto High Street, dead because it was Sunday, and finally found the telephone box.

The operator put me through to Jim Mudd.

"Mudd residence," Jim Mudd said.

"Jim, hi. It's me, it's Keith."

"Don't know I should be talking to you, shag," he said. "I heard what you did to Stake's brother. You and that ponce."

"Look, fuck you, Jim! Alright? Fuck. You. That bastard come looking for me with a screwdriver. What were I gonna do, let him stick it in me? And you can tell Dobbo and all your mates that too."

"Keith…"

"Shut it, Jim, I'll take on any of you skinhead scumbags when the time's right. Bunch of pricks, all of you. Now put Kelly on the bastard telephone."

"I don't like your language or tone, shag. I don't…"

I heard him sigh then shout for Kelly as he muffled the telephone.

I ducked, hoping the coppers didn't come by looking for me.

"What do *you* want?"

"Kelly, I need your help. I'm in the crap."

"What? Why?"

"I need you to say you were gonna meet me last night. When the coppers come round, I need you to say you were gonna spend last night with me at Ryeford Bridge. We were gonna watch the sun come up."

"You're not… You want an alibi?"

"Just say that, OK? You wanted to see the sun come up with me last night at Ryeford Bridge but you couldn't make it. You wanted to but we didn't, OK?"

"Keith, listen to me…"

"Come on Kelly, do this for me and I'll take you to the pictures. Tonight. *Dirty Harry* and *Magnum Force* double-bill at the Regal. On me."

"I don't like…"

"Gimme that," Jim Mudd said, coming on the line.

The pips were going.

"Tell Kelly to say..."

The line went dead and I sank to my knees, head in my hands.

It was getting worse.

Maybe the coppers had Rebecca already?

Fuck that, why would they?

I staggered across the street, getting back to the lock-ups near mine the long way round. There was probably just enough in the tank to get me to the filling station on Tallentyre Way.

Knackered, I started up and roared off in that direction, eyes peeled for coppers all the way. No-one around.

The pump monkey filled her up in record time and I roared off the forecourt, feeling like I'd had a close shave but the worst was behind me.

No-one could get me now.

Ten minutes later, they spotted me on King James Road.

One panda, sirens going on and them tearing up after me.

It overtook, waved me in and screeched to a halt up ahead.

I couldn't run anymore.

It's over, Keith, you tried and you failed, I thought, crapping myself.

The bike stopped and I climbed off, putting my hands up like I was in America or a movie or something.

Only I couldn't believe it.

The out-of-towners from Stanley Street nick. These weren't local coppers, probably weren't looking for me at all. The ones doing the cycling tests from the other day.

"Right then, fella," the same one said. "We meet again. Why have we pulled you over?"

I smiled, out of breath. Get this out of the way and I was free to go, to do a runner as best I could. Piss off to fight another day. In minutes I'd be a man on the lam again. I'd be McQueen in *The Getaway*, no, *The Great Escape* because he had a bike in that. I'd be McQueen with Bowie's hair.

"I'm sorry, constable," I said. "I forgot about…"

"Keith something, weren't it?"

"Yes, constable. Moran. Look."

"No helmet again, Keith Moran. Plus you didn't bring me your licence when I asked for it."

"I couldn't afford the petrol," I said. "I've only just been paid so were gonna bring it today."

"Sounds plausible," Waddicor said. "Maybe you could do with a cycling proficiency test, eh?"

I smiled.

"I suppose you can't afford a helmet yet either?"

"I can now, constable."

He sighed and shook his head. They hadn't heard about me yet, these out-of-towners. They'd have been bouncing me off the bonnet if they had.

I was nearly there.

"You see where we're coming from, don't you, fella?"

I nodded.

"Just this one time, we'll let you off."

"Thank you, constable."

There.

"Now your licence. Let me see it."

Here we go, I thought, reaching for it in my back pocket. They inspect it, they tell you you'll end up in an early grave and they fuck off.

Only...

When she came round on Tuesday I was digging it out but she walked in and...

"It appears I've mislaid it, constable," I said slowly. "But tomorrow, I'll..."

"What a surprise," he said as Waddicor shook his head. "No second chances, fella, we're clamping down. If you don't have it about you, you'll have to come with us."

FOURTEEN

Burning Love

What he did remember was finishing off the Blue Nun and moving onto bottles of Outlaw she had stashed away.

Rebecca slowed her drinking as he accelerated, getting through loads of that vodka.

When he was pissed enough, he made a move on her but she laughed it off.

She told him she was certain he'd help her with her little scheme, he told her no thanks, you're tasty and all that but I didn't jump out of a frying pan to land in your fire.

Again, she told him he'd change his mind.

Again he said he wouldn't.

Promising himself he'd be on the next train anywhere, Heslin rolled over and passed out on her moquette just after midnight.

Before he did though, he remembered, he *definitely* remembered her giving him this strange look as she stood at the door. Like the one in the car – she was studying him or looking through him or something. It gave him that feeling again.

She smiled and went off to bed.

He slept in his clothes.

That's what he did remember.

His mouth was dry and he was definitely hungover. He could feel the sun on his face, on his body all over. He was starting to sweat. Other than the shades covering his eyes, he was naked.

Heslin raised his head and straight away started to panic.

He was lying on the rusty camp bed in her back garden, facing the house. And he couldn't move. His wrists were handcuffed by his sides, ankles the same.

What the Hell was...

"Oi!"

The bitch wasn't around.

Where was she?

"Hey, what's going on? Get me out of these..."

He started to struggle, yanking at the bed without any luck. He tried to ease his wrists out, tried to kick his legs free. "Jesus. Shit! Shit!"

The back door opened and his heart pounded that bit faster when she stepped out.

She was fully clothed, brown top, bare arms, brown flares, flat sandals and that made him feel more naked, more self-conscious, more helpless. And as she came down the grass towards him, he got a good look at what she was carrying.

"Erm, Rebecca," he said, calm as he could. "What do you need cooking oil for?"

I stood by the desk as Luke signed autographs for these fawning coppers, every one of them having an opinion on *Motown Cop* and begging him to get them work on it.

Fair play to him though, his fame got us off the hook. No charges or any of that crap. When he'd finished, we went out onto the steps.

"I never got chance to say it last night," I said, "but cheers for everything. You were brilliant. A proper mate."

"Forget about it," Luke said. "Anyone would have done the same."

"No, they wouldn't, that's the thing. Them bastards had screwdrivers and would have carved me up good and proper if you hadn't stepped in. Thanks mate. Listen, do you wanna come over later? I'll get us some cans."

"Cheers but I'm gonna have a wander back to Rebecca's, let her know we're alright. We're coming over one night anyway, aren't we?"

"Yeah," I said. "Alright, well cheers again. See you."

I went up the street and crossed, rounding a corner and heading for the canal bridge and a short cut home.

Christ, what a night.

I needed a wash so much. And my own bed. And my own bog. No more buckets.

We'd been lucky, thinking about it.

Last night's coppers hadn't been so keen on Kidney and doubly so when they heard he'd been trying to kill the bloke from the telly. The last thing I heard before passing out was him taking a kicking next door and crying out for his brief. These Front types weren't as hard as they thought they were.

As I wandered past the lead factory, I started to wonder whether I should take a proper stand. Like join the International Marxist Group. Or Searchlight. There'd been this tasty blonde bird on the market a few months back handing out leaflets, saying I should join them if I liked soul so much.

Nah, fuck it, I thought, crossing in front of the florist, it's dog eat dog. I'll fight my battles and no-one else's.

I heard her before I saw her.

The roar of the Scimitar, "My Wife" by The Who blaring out of the radio and there she was, shooting past me and grinding to a halt.

Leaning in, I smiled.

She had a face like thunder. "Where the Hell have you been?"

"We got arrested. Me and Luke. Nothing serious, just some…"

"Get in. We need to talk."

I didn't argue. Just got in and got a quick glance at her, looking cool all in white today.

"Where we going?"

She didn't answer and we burned off, back into town.

"Where's Luke?"

"Going back to yours."

"Good."

We came to the junction leading onto Donovan Road and looking left, there was Luke in a telephone box, having a right fit.

"Look," I said.

Rebecca lowered her shades to watch him smack the receiver up and down several times – all violence like last night.

"Let's pick him up," I said. "Hey Lu…!"

"Shut up!" she snapped, hitting me across the chest.

She slammed the Scimitar into reverse and we went back the way we came, her handbraking it to point us in the opposite direction.

"Why can't we pick him up?"

She pushed her shades back up her nose but not before I clocked her black eye.

"What's…?"

"Luke is who I need to see you about," Rebecca said and floored it.

"It's for you," she said, sitting at the small table, crossing her legs and smiling. "Comfortable?"

"Course I'm not bleeding comfortable! Get me out of these!"

She shook her head, drumming her nails on the table.

"Look Rebecca," he said slowly. "If this is some kind of punishment for being fresh then come on, be reasonable. I'm sorry, yeah? I'm sorry. I was drunk, alright?"

"Tut tut. It's nothing to do with that. All I'm doing is enlisting your help."

"What?"

"You should have agreed to help me last night when I first asked," she said. "But you didn't. So this is why it's come to this."

"What are you talking about, you stupid bitch?"

Rebecca stood up and came over to him, kneeling so her face was only inches from his and he could smell her Scherezade. For a moment he wanted to headbutt the cow and break her nose, but knowing if he did he was royally screwed.

Gently stroking his hair, she smiled softly. "You're very newsworthy right now, aren't you?" she whispered. "A lot of people want to know where the movie star is and what he's up to. I imagine they'd print anything that concerns you, don't you?"

"Eh?"

"I have photos," she said, tracing around his lips with her index finger. "I took them while you were passed out here. Luke the movie star all naked and helpless. Imagine if they fell into the wrong hands."

"You're lying."

Rebecca laughed and ran her palms slowly up and down his bare chest. "Who knows where they may end up? Sidney King's desk perhaps? *The News Of The World* maybe? Or even *Health & Efficiency*," she said, standing up and folding her arms. "Imagine the movie star going back to nature. Your reputation – to quote Rod and the boys – would be bigger than gasoline."

"Look," Heslin said. "Just... look. I don't know what I did or why you're doing this but just let me go and I'll be on my way. I won't bother you again."

Rebecca went back to the table, resting her hand on the bottle and laughing.

There was no traffic on the road out to Fairfield Hall and she really opened it up, her mixtape blasting out The Stones, Zep and Elton – which was when she stopped it.

"I miss me music," I said.

She ignored me and we carried on in silence before she pulled into the empty car park at the Hall.

Parking up, she told me to get out and I followed her to the edge of the hill, catching her up as she started to head down to the lake.

"Are you gonna tell me?"

"What happened last night?"

"Skinheads," I shrugged.

By the lake, she parked her arse on a bench, watching the ducks and looking like she wished she'd brought bread.

"What is it?"

"It's Luke," she said, not looking at me. "You were right about him."

I sat next to her, staring at her profile, no idea what she was thinking.

"I should never have got him to come in with us. It should have stayed you and I. I was wrong."

"What happened to your eye?"

"He hit me. On Tuesday when I got back from yours."

"Why'd he hit you?"

"Because he's a bastard," she said. "A wicked, selfish bastard. Handy with his fists, as you probably know by now."

"Yeah. Look…"

"He's planning to double-cross you, Keith. He's been with us three days and he's planning on getting your share and said if I told you, he'd… cut me. He's an animal."

"You what?"

Never. Not after last night. We were mates now.

"I don't know what he's planning but *this* is what he gave me to prove he means business."

"He can't get one over on me," I said. "Not me. I'm sharper than I look. No way is he having my share. Fuck that."

I was staring into the water when I felt her hand caress my neck. "Keith," she said softly. "You're going to have to kill him."

"I've spent a long time planning this to the nth degree. When I saw you last night and heard your tale of woe, I knew you'd be perfect for it. This is merely to show you what a bitch I can be."

"You seriously need some bloody help, Rebecca."

"I have you," she said, straddling him and flicking the top off the bottle.

She poured a liberal amount onto his chest – its coldness making him wince – and she began to rub it in slowly. All over from his shoulders and his neck right down to his waistline and up his sides.

He kept silent, kept dignified, didn't want her to see how terrified he was of this mad bitch, humming to herself.

She had photos.

Oh shit...

If Sid didn't finish his career then there was every chance this nutjob giving him the world's most messed up massage would.

"There we go," she said, patting his chest. "Now you're done." With a laugh, she stood up and went back to the table. "I'll set up a meeting for you and Keith. And don't look so angry, you're about to embark on a criminal career that'll make you rich. Surely that's worth a few hours of discomfort?"

"*Hours,*" he snapped. "You're not..."

He shut up and shook his head. She turned her back on him and walked to the house, saying over her shoulder, "Besides, you'll have a real movie star tan when you're healed."

Heslin glared as she went inside and began to wash her hands at the sink.

He wished to God he'd never stepped into that bloody pub.

"No way. No fuckin' way. I'm not killing him for you or anyone. Not killing him for myself either."

Christ, this was madness. The way she said it so casually, 'kill him' like it was the most natural thing in the world. 'Kill him.' Kill the bloke from *Motown Cop*. Yeah, because it's so simple and so easy and murderers never get caught or anything.

"Are you stupid?" I said. "I'm not... Why have you even...? Cos he blacked your eye?"

"Because I know that if you don't do it to him, he'll do it to you," she said, stroking my neck as she spoke.

"You don't know anything."

"It's what he said. That factory's a death trap, plenty of places to leave you to burn. I'm warning you, Keith. Please."

"Fuck off."

"When that safe's open and he's got the money..."

"Look, fuck off. Alright?"

Rebecca took her shades off and looked right into my eyes, pleading yet... ordering me too. It seemed like she wasn't asking, she was telling me to do something she knew I'd do anyway.

I shook my head. "No. Sorry. And you shouldn't go round saying things like that. Nothing about this kind of crap when we first got talking. Killing. Fuck you *and* the money."

"The money?" she sneered. "Pathetic. You're putting morals before money for once."

"Yeah. I am. I'm starting to do good things, I'm starting to…"

"OK."

"What?"

"OK."

"What does that…? Look, me and him are cool now, I'll speak to him. Killing…"

She broke into a smile then laughed and stood up, walking down the path.

"What are you laughing at? Were that a joke? Were it?" I caught her up and took her elbow. "You were joking?"

"No," she said, standing still. "Not at all."

"Then…"

"I know him better than you," she said. "I know what he's capable of and how badly he wants this to go right. And knowing all this, do you know what else I know?" She was so calm, arms folded, drumming her fingers up and down. "I know that there's only one of you who will walk away from that factory alive. The funny thing is, you're the one with the choice and you won't take it."

She nodded up the hill and told me I could walk home then she carried on towards the bridge.

I just watched her.

He was starting to redden and itch and the sun wasn't even at its highest yet. He wanted to scratch or put cold water on his chest or anything and all the writhing and struggling in the world wouldn't do him any good.

She had him, photos or not.

Rebecca came out of the house minutes later, driving gloves on, putting her handbag on the table.

"I have to go see Keith now," she said. "Depending on how well you're fried when I return, I might let you go."

"You should probably know that the minute you do, I'm gonna black your eyes."

"Although I might mow the lawn first if you're going to be like that. The grass is getting a bit too long for my liking. Maybe even clean out the pond. Or perhaps you could do that for me?"

"Are you deaf?" he snapped. "I'm not doing anything for you."

She laughed and smiled down at him, almost tenderly. "You know, I do have a softer side," she said. "And when I've finished with you, you'll do anything I ask."

"Piss off."

Without taking her eyes from his, she put her shades on the table, kneeling again, but this time further down, taking his cock in her hand and kissing the end softly.

Heslin sighed and laid back not knowing how in the world all this was gonna pan out or how his messed up life had come to this.

When she finished, he shot his head back in ecstasy, writhing as best he could, feeling that sun burn his chest and looking down to see her swallow.

Taking her bag from the table, she asked him in a soft voice 'for the last time' whether he was gonna help her with her little scheme, saying she'd explain the details when she returned.

He lifted his head and nodded, the pleasure disappearing, and the fear of the painful afternoon he was about to have setting in.

She was so screwed up, he couldn't say no.

"Good boy," Rebecca said. "Now lie back and relax."

She put her bag on her shoulder, flicked her hair and laughed at the movie star who'd fallen into her trap.

I put the car radio on when we got back, my heart still pounding and me needing to hear someone else's voice after the last hour of just me and her.

"Breaking news now," a man was saying, "and in a surprise move announced only this morning, Norman Browning has stated that he will not be selling up his paint factory to clear alleged gambling debts."

It *was* a dog eat dog world…

"Workers and unions were worried this would lead to a loss of around fifteen hundred jobs. Rumours have been rife for weeks now that the factory would be bulldozed to make way for a housing estate."

And if it was between the two of us…

"I wonder what the man himself has to say," Rebecca muttered.

"It were never my intention to sell the factory nor were it my intention to make my private business public."

I could have taken Kidney and his mates without his help…

"I believe that the lies and misinformation spread among my workforce were a calculated plot by the TGWU designed to undermine my authority and bring production of paint in the north this country to a complete halt."

It wasn't as if I made him shaft his career. He did that himself and now he was on *my* turf, muscling in on *my* scheme with his sharp suit and double-crossing, backstabbing bastard ways.

Fuck you, Luke, throwing it in my face. Well, we'll see who's the top dog, won't we?

"However, I will be putting this business behind me now and look forward to forging ahead with my employees to create a brighter future."

"I thought Luke were me mate."

"Scum like him don't want mates, Keith," Rebecca said, turning the radio off. "Now come on, there are thousands of pounds sitting in that safe. Enough to set us both up for a brighter future, in the words of Mr. Browning. All you have to do is kill for it."

FIFTEEN

What Dorothy Saw

What was the final straw?

Christ, what *was* the final straw?

Was it Kidney, real name Mr. Nigel Stakeley, getting up for the Prosecution, saying what a vicious little bastard I was and then giving me a wink on his way out?

Maybe it was that copper from the desk, Sergeant Robert Harmon, telling the jury about my foul mouth and refusing to play Sparks at his wedding.

Or Mr. Guotin Li from Hing Lung getting his fifteen minutes, saying I'd blackmailed him into giving me a free feed every night – my only good deed being used against me for fuck's sake.

Jim Mudd perhaps? Mr. James Mudd telling the local paper I was a three time killer: Aldo, Luke and Kelly's kid.

How about Station Officer Clyde Prior from the Fire Brigade, whose officers had been hospitalised with breathing difficulties, saying I'd turned that factory into a death trap for them all?

Was the final straw when I was sitting in my cell after a four-hour beating, thinking how funny they all found it that I'd have got away if I'd had my licence on me?

Any one of these could have been the final straw, the one that broke the camel's back.

On their own, they meant nothing, but add them onto what the suits from Regional Crime Squad told me one morning a few days before my trial and you'll see why I did what I did.

"So let's get this straight, Mr. Moran," Wolverstone said as Irish lit their cigars. "She approached you. You were friendly but never slept with her. Yet somehow she persuaded you into helping her frame Mr. Browning. Correct?"

I'd already made my mind up I was gonna sing. She could have turned herself in and helped me out but oh no, she'd fucked off somewhere, wherever, to put weight on and get a tan.

"Yeah," I said. "You want me to sum it up? *Again?*"

"Succinctly, son," Irish said, lighting up. "It means without the punctuation."

"March fifteenth, OK? Norman Browning runs over her bloke. Fred Dryden. He kills him and drives off. You lot fit up a perv for it cos Browning's too powerful and too ambitious to send down."

Wolverstone was smiling, Irish looking like he wanted to throw me through the wall.

"So she wants her own back. First off: rob the bastard."

"Watch your mouth."

"Then destroy the factory, make it look like an inside job. We get rich on the payroll, he goes to claim the insurance but they don't pay out cos it looks dodgy.

Add to that he were on about selling the land but then he backs out a few days before the place goes up. There you have it. The claims blokes move in, he can't prove it weren't him and they send him down."

"That is *brilliant*."

"Your idea, son?"

"Hers."

"Whose?"

"Rebecca's."

"Rebecca who?"

I glared at them, thinking, how could they not know her name? She was infamous. "Lady Scimitar" *The Evening Standard* had named her.

"Rebecca Rollins."

Irish reached into an envelope and pulled out a photo, putting it face down on the table. "Have a look at that and tell me if that's her."

I flipped it over and shook my head.

This was a woman about eighty or ninety, standing outside a bungalow, squinting or smiling, I couldn't tell. "Course it's not her, she were about thirty. How have you...?"

Something wasn't right.

"She's the only Rebecca Rollins on the Electoral Roll in a hundred mile radius, son."

"You what?"

"And she were found beaten to death in her home last Christmas."

I froze and that sweat started to travel down my spine. They were both giving me their *Motown Cop* looks. Interrogation looks.

"Rebecca won't have..."

"Maybe not," Wolverstone said. "Maybe she didn't kill this Miss Rollins' gardener either."

"One Mr. Frederick Dryden," Irish said, taking a drag.

"What the fuck?"

Oh Christ, what was all this about?

Who was Rebecca if she wasn't Rebecca Rollins?

"Just names, son," Irish said. "She's just someone who reads the papers when she plots things like this."

Wolverstone turned to Irish and folded his arms. "If Mr. Moran asks me who Mr. Browning did kill on March fifteenth, I might throw this table at him."

Then he turned back and smiled.

I bit my lip.

"Tell him, guv," Irish said. "Don't keep him in suspense."

"Alright," Wolverstone said. "No-one. He killed no-one."

"Weren't even in the country."

"Business trip."

"No Rebecca, no Fred, no death," Irish said, stubbing out his fag on the floor. "You really should have made an effort to see this bitch's house, son."

"Can I have some water?" I said. "I think I'm gonna faint."

"I read the report on you this morning," Wolverstone said. "They reckon you're down in the dumps."

"They think I might kill myself."

"Depression, eh? Y'know, Mr. Irish and I used to have a saying, back in the day. Mr. Irish came up with it. He's an Elmore James fan. It's his way of saying – actually – Mr. Irish will tell you."

"Hangmen," Irish said, lighting another, leaning on the wall. "Even they get the blues."

"Wonderful, isn't it?" Wolverstone beamed. "You understand the concept? No matter how tough you are, you...? Course you get it."

"Chin up, son," Irish said. "It's not all bad news. Tell him, guv."

Wolverstone folded his hands under his chin and gazed at me, smiling.

"The water?" I said.

"There's a very good reason you're in here, Mr. Moran."

"Insurance scam, you said?" Irish murmured. "The oldest trick in the book, son."

"It happened in Market Drayton in seventy-one. Glasgow in sixty-nine."

"An ailing business about to go tits up."

"The owner pleads ignorance."

"All doe-eyed."

"Nothing can be proved."

"Robbery and arson?" Wolverstone said.

"It's neither," Irish said, blowing out smoke.

"It's fraud."

"I don't get it," I said.

"The thing about old tricks, Mr. Moran..."

"Is that only young 'uns fall for 'em."

"You what?"

"Your statement, dated September second nineteen seventy-four. You said Miss Rollins, in inverted commas, owned an orange Reliant Scimitar. A seventy-three model. Is that correct?"

"Yeah."

"I want you to tell us everything you know about that woman. *Everything*. All of it."

"Again? Why should I?"

Wolverstone leant forward, fixing me with his gaze. "Because we think it's strange that now Mr. Browning's insurance claim has gone through, he's not home anymore."

"Stranger still," said Irish, "that he were allegedly spotted by a Mrs. Dorothy Hammond, leaving a Bureau de Change three hundred miles down south..."

"Crossing the road..."

"Taking care to look both ways..."

"And being driven away in a bright orange seventy-three Scimitar."

I sat up.

"Mrs. Hammond recognised the car from the papers, son," Irish said, crushing his fag on the floor and checking his pockets for another.

"He's neither been seen nor heard of since. What do you make of that?"

"What do I...?"

No way...

"Insurance," I said. "He *did* do it for the insurance. Only it were him and her... She... They're rich on..."

"So, Rebecca or whatever her name is gives you a story to hook you. One so easy for him to deny *with evidence* and us to disprove, that you look like the class clown and he can't be charged at all. Only, on the strength of one nosy old cow's peeping – something we're checking by the way – we can *deduce* that maybe he did do it for the insurance. With a little help from a tart and two glove puppets."

169

I slammed my head down onto the table, closing my eyes and feeling sick.

"Bright lad," Irish muttered. "You got a light, guv?"

But even that wasn't the final straw, oh no.

In fact, by the time they got round to telling me it, I was so numb and so fucked in the head, I'd almost come to expect something like that.

They walked me back to my cell, Irish saying maybe there was a Rebecca in every man's life, sent to test him? The measure of man you were was gained from how well you did in this test, whether you passed it or not or some such blues bullshit.

No, the final straw was them finding my records safe and sound on Redhouse Market one Sunday morning after I got life. They traced them back and it turned out I was burgled by him from the Star Of India. Revenge for the kicking I gave him over knocking up Kelly. You wouldn't think with all the other shit I was swimming in, that would be the final straw.

But really it was.

It got to me so bad that they found me in a pool of blood the next morning, 'dog eat dog' finally floating out of my mind after going round and round like a fucking broken record all night.

John Featherstone
Brief Biography

John Featherstone was born in Doncaster and studied Film & Literature at Sheffield Hallam University. His first novel, *Sergio's Exile*, was written in 2006. He followed this up with *Hangman's Got The Blues* in 2009 and expects to complete his third and fourth novels in 2011. At present, he lives and writes in Sheffield.

Lightning Source UK Ltd.
Milton Keynes UK
22 July 2010

157350UK00001B/55/P